HORRID HENRY

RULES THE SCHOOL

Meet HORRiD HENRY
the laugh-out-loud
worldwide sensation!

★ Over 15 million copies sold in 27
   countries and counting

★ # 1 chapter book series in the UK

★ Francesca Simon is the only American
   author to ever win the Galaxy British
   Book Awards Children's Book of the
   year (past winners include J. K. Rowling,
   Philip Pullman, and Eoin Colfer).

"I have tried out the Horrid Henry books with groups of children as a parent, as a baby-sitter, and as a teacher. **Children love to either hear them read aloud or to read them themselves**." —Danielle Hall, teacher

"A flicker of recognition must pass through most teachers and parents when they read Horrid Henry. **There's a tiny bit of him in all of us**." —Nancy Astee, *Child Education*

"**As a teacher...it's great to get a series of books my class loves**. They go mad for Horrid Henry." —teacher

"**Short, easy-to-read chapters will appeal to early readers, who will laugh at Henry's exaggerated antics and relate to his rambunctious personality**." —*School Library Journal*

"An absolutely fantastic series and surely a winner with all children. Long live Francesca Simon and her brilliant books! More, more please!"

—parent

"Laugh-out-loud reading for both adults and children alike." —parent

"**Henry's over-the-top behavior, the characters' snappy dialogue and Ross's hyperbolic line art will engage even the most reluctant readers—there's little reason to suspect the series won't conquer these shores as well**." —*Publishers Weekly*

Horrid Henry by Francesca Simon

Horrid Henry

Horrid Henry Tricks the Tooth Fairy

Horrid Henry and the Mega-Mean Time Machine

Horrid Henry's Stinkbomb

Horrid Henry and the Mummy's Curse

Horrid Henry and the Soccer Fiend

Horrid Henry's Underpants

Horrid Henry and the Scary Sitter

Horrid Henry's Christmas

Horrid Henry and the Abominable Snowman

Horrid Henry Rocks

Horrid Henry Wakes the Dead

Horrid Henry's Joke Book

Horrid Henry Rules the School

Horrid Henry's Friends and Enemies

HORRID HENRY

RULES THE SCHOOL

Francesca Simon
Illustrated by Tony Ross

sourcebooks
jabberwocky

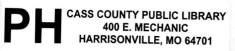

"Horrid Henry's New Teacher" originally appeared in *Horrid Henry Tricks the Tooth Fairy*, text © Francesca Simon 1996, illustrations © Tony Ross 1996

"Horrid Henry's Homework" and "Horrid Henry's Swimming Lesson" originally appeared in *Horrid Henry and the Mummy's Curse*, text © Francesca Simon 2000, illustrations © Tony Ross 2000

"Horrid Henry's School Project" and "Horrid Henry Reads a Book" originally appeared in *Horrid Henry's Stinkbomb*, text © Francesca Simon 2002, illustrations © Tony Ross 2002

"Horrid Henry's Underpants" and "Horrid Henry's Sick Day" originally appeared in *Horrid Henry's Underpants*, text © Francesca Simon 2003, illustrations © Tony Ross 2003

"Horrid Henry's Author Visit" originally appeared in *Horrid Henry and the Abominable Snowman*, text © Francesca Simon 2007, illustrations © Tony Ross 2007

"Horrid Henry's Dance Class" originally appeared in *Horrid Henry*, text © Francesca Simon 1994, illustrations © Tony Ross 1994

"Horrid Henry and the Soccer Fiend" originally appeared in *Horrid Henry and the Soccer Fiend*, text © Francesca Simon 2006, illustrations © Tony Ross 2006

Jokes originally appeared in *Horrid Henry's Joke Book*, text © Francesca Simon 2004, illustrations © Tony Ross 2004

Cover and internal design © 2011 by Sourcebooks, Inc.
Sourcebooks and the colophon are registered trademarks of Sourcebooks, Inc.

Published by Sourcebooks Jabberwocky, an imprint of Sourcebooks, Inc.
P.O. Box 4410, Naperville, Illinois 60567-4410
(630) 961-3900
Fax: (630) 961-2168
www.jabberwockykids.com

Library of Congress Cataloging-in-Publication data is on file with the publisher.

Source of Production: Versa Press, East Peoria, Illinois, USA
Date of Production: May 2011
Run Number: 15101

Printed and bound in the United States of America.
VP 10 9 8 7 6 5 4 3 2 1

CONTENTS

HORRID HENRY'S NEW TEACHER

....

"Now Henry," said Dad. "Today is the first day of school. A chance for a fresh start with a new teacher."

"Yeah, yeah," scowled Horrid Henry.

He hated the first day of school. Another year, another teacher to show who was boss. His first teacher, Miss Marvel, had run screaming from the classroom after two weeks. His next teacher, Mrs. Zip, had run screaming from the classroom after one day. Breaking in new teachers wasn't easy, thought Henry, but someone had to do it.

Dad got out a piece of paper and waved it.

"Henry, I never want to read another report card like this again," he said. "Why can't your report cards be like Peter's?"

Henry started whistling.

"Pay attention, Henry," shouted Dad. "This is important. Look at this report card."

HENRY'S REPORT CARD

It has been horrible Teaching Henry this year. He is rude, lazy, and disruptive. The worst student I have ever taught.

Behavior: Horrid

English: Horrid

Math: Horrid

Science: Horrid

P.E.: Horrid

"What about *my* report card?" said
Perfect Peter.

Dad beamed.

"Your report card was perfect, Peter,"
said Dad. "Keep up the wonderful work."

PETER'S REPORT CARD

It has been a pleasure
teaching Peter this year. He is
polite, hardworking, and
cooperative. The best student I
have ever taught.

Behavior: Perfect

English: Perfect

Math: Perfect

Science: Perfect

P.E.: Perfect

Peter smiled proudly.

"You'll just have to try harder, Henry,"
said Peter, smirking.

Horrid Henry was a shark sinking his teeth into a drowning sailor.

"OWWWW," shrieked Peter. "Henry bit me!"

"Don't be horrid, Henry!" shouted Dad. "Or no TV for a week."

"I don't care," muttered Henry. When he became king he'd make it a law that parents, not children, had to go to school.

Horrid Henry pushed and shoved his way into class and grabbed the seat next to Rude Ralph.

"Nah nah ne nah nah, I've got a new football," said Ralph.

Henry didn't have a football. He'd kicked his through Moody Margaret's window.

"Who cares?" said Horrid Henry.

The classroom door slammed. It was

Mr. Nerdon, the toughest, meanest, nastiest teacher in the school.

"SILENCE!" he said, glaring at them with his bulging eyes. "I don't want to hear a sound. I don't even want to hear anyone breathe."

The class held its breath.

"GOOD!" he growled. "I'm Mr. Nerdon."

Henry snorted. What a stupid name.

"Nerd," he whispered to Ralph.

Rude Ralph giggled.

"Nerdy Nerd," whispered Horrid Henry, snickering.

Mr. Nerdon walked up to Henry and jabbed his finger in his face.

"Quiet, you horrible boy!" said Mr. Nerdon. "I've got my eye on you. Oh yes. I've heard about your other teachers. Bah! I'm made of stronger stuff. There will be no nonsense in *my* class."

We'll see about that, thought Henry.

"Our first math problems for the year are on the board. Now get to work," ordered Mr. Nerdon.

Horrid Henry had an idea.

Quickly he scribbled a note to Ralph.

Ralph – I bet you that I can make Mr. Nerdon run screaming out of class by the end of lunchtime.

No way, Henry

If I do will you give me your new football?

O.K. But if you don't, you have to give me a dollar.

O.K.

Horrid Henry took a deep breath and went to work. He rolled up some paper, stuffed it in his mouth, and spat it out. The spitball whizzed through the air and pinged Mr. Nerdon on the back of his neck.

Mr. Nerdon wheeled round.

"You!" snapped Mr. Nerdon. "Don't you mess with me!"

"It wasn't *me!*" said Henry. "It was Ralph."

"Liar!" said Mr. Nerdon. "Sit at the back of the class."

Horrid Henry moved his seat next to Clever Clare.

"Move over, Henry!" hissed Clare. "You're on my side of the desk."

Henry shoved her.

"Move over yourself," he hissed back.

Then Horrid Henry reached over and broke Clare's pencil.

"Henry broke my pencil!" shrieked Clare.

Mr. Nerdon moved Henry next to Weepy William.

Henry pinched him.

Mr. Nerdon moved Henry next to Tough Toby.

Henry jiggled the desk.

Mr. Nerdon moved Henry next to Lazy Linda.

Henry scribbled all over her paper.

Mr. Nerdon moved Henry next to Moody Margaret.

Moody Margaret drew a line down the middle of the desk.

"Cross that line, Henry, and you're dead," said Margaret under her breath.

Henry looked up. Mr. Nerdon was writing spelling words on the board.

Henry started to erase Margaret's line.

"Stop it, Henry," said Mr. Nerdon, without turning round.

Henry stopped.

Mr. Nerdon continued writing.

Henry pulled Margaret's hair.

Mr. Nerdon moved Henry next to Beefy Bert, the biggest boy in the class.

Beefy Bert was chewing his pencil and trying to add 2 + 2 without much luck.

Horrid Henry inched his chair onto Beefy Bert's side of the desk.

Bert ignored him.

Henry poked him.

Bert ignored him.

Henry hit him.

POW!

The next thing Henry knew he was lying on the floor, looking up at the ceiling. Beefy Bert continued chewing his pencil.

"What happened, Bert?" said Mr. Nerdon.

"I dunno," said Beefy Bert.

"Get up off the floor, Henry!" said Mr. Nerdon. A faint smile appeared on the teacher's slimy lips.

"He hit me!" said Henry. He'd never felt such a punch in his life.

"It was an accident," said Mr. Nerdon. He smirked. "You'll sit next to Bert from now on."

That's it, thought Henry. Now it's war.

"How absurd, to be a nerdy bird," said Horrid Henry behind Mr. Nerdon's back.

Slowly Mr. Nerdon turned and walked toward him. His hand was clenched into a fist.

"Since you're so good at rhyming," said Mr. Nerdon. "Everyone write a poem. Now."

Henry slumped in his seat and groaned. A poem! Yuck! He hated poems. Even the word *poem* made him want to throw up.

Horrid Henry caught Rude Ralph's eye. Ralph was grinning and mouthing,

"A dollar, a dollar!" at him. Time
was running out. Despite Henry's best
efforts, Mr. Nerdon still hadn't run
screaming from the class. Henry would
have to act fast to get that football.

What horrible poem could he write?
Horrid Henry smiled. Quickly he
picked up his pencil and went to work.

"Now, who's my first victim?" said Mr.
Nerdon. He looked around the room.
"Susan! Read your poem."

Sour Susan stood up and read:

> "Bow wow
> Bow wow
> Woof woof woof
> I'm a dog, not a cat, so…
> SCAT!"

13

"Not enough rhymes," said Mr. Nerdon. "Next…" He looked round the room. "Graham!"

Greedy Graham stood up and read:

"Chocolate chocolate chocolate sweet,
Cakes and doughnuts can't be beat.
Ice cream is my favorite treat
With lots and lots of pie to eat!"

"Too many rhymes," said Mr. Nerdon. "Next…" He scowled at the class. Henry tried to look as if he didn't want the teacher to call on him.

"Henry!" snapped Mr. Nerdon. "Read your poem!"

Horrid Henry stood up and read:

"Pirates puke on stormy seas,
Giants spew on top of trees."

14

Henry peeked at Mr. Nerdon. He
looked pale. Henry continued to read:

"Kings are sick in golden bowls,
Dogs throw up on Dad's casseroles."

Henry peeked again at Mr. Nerdon.
He looked green. Any minute now,
thought Henry, and he'll be out of here
screaming. He read on:

"Babies love to make a mess,
Down the front of Mom's best dress.

And what car ride would be complete,
Without the stink of last night's treat?"

"That's enough," choked Mr.
Nerdon. "Wait, I haven't got to the
good part," said Horrid Henry.

"I said that's enough!" gasped Mr.
Nerdon. "You fail."

He made a big black mark in his book.

"I threw up on the boat!" shouted
Greedy Graham.

"I threw up on the plane!" shouted
Sour Susan.

"I threw up in the car!" shouted
Dizzy Dave.

"I said that's enough!" ordered Mr.
Nerdon. He glared at Horrid Henry.
"Get out of here, all of you! It's
lunchtime."

Rats, thought Henry. Mr. Nerdon was
one tough teacher.

Rude Ralph grabbed him.

"Ha ha, Henry," said Ralph. "You lose. Gimme that dollar."

"No," said Henry. "I've got until the end of lunch."

"You can't do anything to him between now and then," said Ralph.

"Oh yeah?" said Henry. "Just watch me."

Then Henry had a wonderful, spectacular idea. This was it. The best plan he'd ever had. Someday someone would stick a plaque on the school wall celebrating Henry's genius. There would be songs written about him. He'd probably even get a medal. But first things first. In order for his plan to work to perfection, he needed Peter.

Perfect Peter was playing hopscotch with his friends Tidy Ted and Spotless Sam.

"Hey Peter," said Henry. "How would you like to be a real member of the Purple Hand?"

The Purple Hand was Horrid Henry's secret club. Peter had wanted to join for ages, but naturally Henry would never let him.

Peter's jaw dropped open.

"Me?" said Peter.

"Yes," said Henry. "If you can pass the secret club test."

"What do I have to do?" said Peter eagerly.

"It's tricky," said Henry. "And probably much too hard for you."

"Tell me, tell me," said Peter.

"All you have to do is lie down right there below that window and stay absolutely still. You can't move until I tell you to."

"Why?" said Peter.

18

"Because that's the test," said Henry.

Perfect Peter thought for a moment.

"Are you going to drop something on me?"

"No," said Henry.

"OK," said Peter. He lay down obediently.

"And I need your shoes," said Henry.

"Why?" said Peter.

Henry scowled.

"Do you want to be in the secret club or not?" said Henry.

"I do," said Peter.

"Then give me your shoes and be quiet," said Henry. "I'll be checking on you. If I see you moving one little bit, you can't be in my club."

Peter gave Henry his sneakers, then lay still as a statue.

Horrid Henry grabbed the shoes, then dashed up the stairs to his classroom.

It was empty. Good.

Horrid Henry went over to the window and opened it. Then he stood there, holding one of Peter's shoes in each hand.

Henry waited until he heard Mr. Nerdon's footsteps. Then he went into action.

"Help!" shouted Horrid Henry. "Help!"

Mr. Nerdon entered. He saw Henry and glowered.

"What are you doing here? Get out!"

"Help!" shouted Henry. "I can't hold on to him much longer…he's slipping… aaahhh, he's fallen!"

Horrid Henry held up the empty shoes.

"He's gone," whispered Henry. He peeked out of the window. "Ugghh, I can't look."

Mr. Nerdon went pale. He ran to the window and saw Perfect Peter lying still and shoeless on the ground below.

"Oh no," gasped Mr. Nerdon.

"I'm sorry," panted Henry. "I tried to hold on to him, honest, I—"

"Help!" screamed Mr. Nerdon. He raced down the stairs. "Police! Fire! Ambulance! Help! Help!"

He ran over to Peter and knelt by his still body.

"Can I get up now, Henry?" said Perfect Peter.

"What!?" gasped Mr. Nerdon. "What did you say?"

Then the terrible truth dawned. He, Ninius Nerdon, had been tricked.

"YOU HORRID BOY! GO STRAIGHT TO THE PRINCIPAL— NOW!" screeched Mr. Nerdon.

Perfect Peter jumped to his feet.

"But…but—" spluttered Perfect Peter.

"Now!" screamed Mr. Nerdon. "How dare you! To the principal!"

"AAAGGGHHHH," shrieked Peter.

He slunk off to the principal's office, weeping.

Mr. Nerdon turned to race up the stairs to grab Henry.

"I'll get you, Henry!" he screamed. His face was white. He looked as if he were going to faint.

"Help," squeaked Mr. Nerdon.

Then he fainted.

Clunk! Thunk! Thud!

NEE NAW NEE NAW NEE NAW.

When the ambulance arrived, the only person lying on the ground was Mr. Nerdon. They scooped him onto a stretcher and took him away.

The perfect end to a perfect day, thought Horrid Henry, throwing his new football in the air. Peter sent home in disgrace. Mr. Nerdon gone for good. Even the news that scary Miss Battle-Axe would be teaching Henry's class didn't bother him. After all, tomorrow was another day.

HORRiD HENRY'S HOMEWORK

....

Ahhhh, thought Horrid Henry. He
turned on the TV and stretched out.
School was over. What could be better
than lying on the sofa all afternoon, eating
chips and watching TV? Wasn't life great?

Then Mom came in. She did not
look like a mom who thought life was
grand. She looked like a mom on the
warpath against boys who lay on sofas all
afternoon, eating chips and watching TV.

"Get your feet off the sofa, Henry!"
said Mom.

"Unh," grunted Henry.

"Stop getting chips everywhere!"
snapped Mom.

"Unh," grunted Henry.

"Have you done your homework, Henry?" said Mom.

Henry didn't answer.

"HENRY!" shouted Mom.

"WHAT!" shouted Henry.

"Have you done your homework?"

"What homework?" said Henry. He kept his eyes glued to the TV.

"Go, Mutants!" he screeched.

"The five spelling words you are supposed to learn tonight," said Mom.

"Oh," said Henry. "That homework."

Horrid Henry hated homework. He had far better things to do with his precious time than learn how to spell "zipper" or work out the answer to 6×7. For weeks Henry's homework sheets had ended up in the recycling box until Dad found them. Henry swore he had no idea how they got there and blamed Fluffy the cat, but since then Mom and Dad had checked his school bag every day.

Mom snatched the remote and switched off the TV.

"Hey, I'm watching!" said Henry.

"When are you going to do your homework, Henry?" said Mom.

"SOON!" screamed Henry. He'd just returned from a long, hard day at school. Couldn't he have any peace around here? When he was king anyone who said the word "homework" would get thrown to the crocodiles.

"I had a phone call today from Miss Battle-Axe," said Mom. "She said you got a zero in the last ten spelling tests."

"That's not my fault," said Henry. "First I lost the words, then I forgot, then I couldn't read my writing, then I copied the words wrong, then—"

"I don't want to hear any more silly excuses," said Mom. "Do you know your spelling words for tomorrow?"

"Yes," lied Henry.

"Where's the list?" Mom asked.

"I don't know," said Henry.

"Find it or no TV for a month," said Mom.

"It's not fair," muttered Henry, digging the crumpled spelling list out of his pocket.

Mom looked at it.

"There's going to be a test tomorrow," she said. "How do you spell 'goat'?"

"Don't you know how, Mom?" asked Henry.

"Henry..." said Mom.

Henry scowled.

"I'm busy," moaned Henry. "I promise I'll tell you right after *Mutant Madman*. It's my favorite show."

"How do you spell 'goat'?" said Mom.

"G-O-T-E," snapped Henry.

"Wrong," said Mom. "What about 'boat'?"

"Why do I have to do this?" wailed Henry.

"Because it's your homework," said Mom. "You have to learn how to spell."

"But why?" said Henry. "I never write letters."

"Because," said Mom. "Now spell "boat."

"B-O-T-T-E," said Henry.

"No more TV until you do your homework," said Mom.

"I've done all *my* homework," said Perfect Peter. "In fact, I enjoyed it so much I've already done tomorrow's homework as well."

Henry pounced on Peter. He was a cannibal tenderizing his victim for the pot.

"Eeeeyowwww!" screamed Peter.

"Henry! Go to your room!" shouted Mom. "And don't come out until you know *all* your spelling words!"

Horrid Henry stomped upstairs and

slammed his bedroom door. This was
so unfair! He was far too busy to bother
with stupid, boring, useless spelling. For
instance, he hadn't read the new *Mutant
Madman* comic book. He hadn't finished
drawing that treasure map. And he
hadn't even begun to organize his new
collection of Twizzle cards. Homework
would have to wait.

There was just one problem. Miss
Battle-Axe had said that everyone
who spelled all their words correctly
tomorrow would get a pack of Big
Bopper candy. Henry loved Big Bopper
candy. Mom and Dad hardly ever let
him have them. But why on earth did
he have to learn spelling words to get
some? If *he* were the teacher, he'd only
give candy to children who couldn't
spell. Henry sighed. He'd just have to sit
down and learn those stupid words.

4:30. Mom burst into the room. Henry was lying on his bed reading a comic.

"Henry! Why aren't you doing your homework?" said Mom.

"I'll do it in a sec," said Henry. "I'm just finishing this page."

"Henry…" said Mom.

Henry put down the comic.

Mom left. Henry picked up the comic.

5:30. Dad burst into the room. Henry was playing with his knights.

"Henry! Why aren't you doing your homework?" said Dad.

"I'm tired!" yawned Henry. "I'm just taking a little break. It's hard having so much work!"

"Henry, you've only got five words to learn!" said Dad. "And you've just spent two hours *not* learning them."

"All right," snarled Henry. Slowly, he picked up his spelling list. Then he put it down again. He had to get in the mood. Soothing music, that's what he needed. Horrid Henry switched on his radio. The terrible sound of the Driller Cannibals boomed through the house.

"OH, I'M A CAN-CAN- CANNIBAL!" screamed Henry, stomping around his room. "DON'T CALL ME AN ANIMAL JUST 'CAUSE I'M A CAN-CAN- CANNIBAL!"

Mom and Dad stormed into Henry's bedroom and turned off the music.

"That's enough, Henry!" said Dad.

"DO YOUR HOMEWORK!" screamed Mom.

"IF YOU DON'T GET EVERY SINGLE WORD RIGHT IN YOUR TEST TOMORROW THERE

WILL BE NO TELEVISION FOR A
WEEK!" shouted Dad.

EEEK! No TV *and* no candy! This
was too much. Horrid Henry looked at
his spelling words with loathing.

GOAT

BOAT

SAID

STOAT

FRIEND

"I hate goats! I'll never need to spell
the word 'goat' in my life," said Henry.
He hated goat's cheese. He hated goat's
milk. He thought goats were smelly.

That was one word he'd definitely
never need to know.

The next word was "boat." Who
needs to spell that? thought Henry. I'm
not going to be a sailor when I grow
up. I get seasick. In fact, it's bad for my
health to learn how to spell "boat."

As for "said," what did it matter if
he spelled it "sed"? It was perfectly
understandable, written "sed." Only an
old fusspot like Miss Battle-Axe would
mind such a tiny mistake.

Then there was "stoat." What on
earth was a stoat? What a mean, sneaky
word. Henry wouldn't know a stoat if

it sat on him. Of all the useless, horrible words, "stoat" was the worst. Trust his teacher, Miss Battle-Axe, to make him learn a horrible, useless word like stoat.

The last word was "friend." Well, a real friend like Rude Ralph didn't care how the word "friend" was spelled. As far as Henry was concerned any friend who minded how he spelled "friend" was no friend. Miss Battle-Axe included that word to torture him.

Five whole spelling words. It was too much. I'll never learn so many words, thought Henry. But what about tomorrow? He'd have to watch Moody Margaret and Jolly Josh and Clever Clare chomping away at those delicious Big Boppers, while he, Henry, had to gnash his empty teeth. Plus no TV for a week! Henry couldn't live that long without TV!

He was sunk. He was doomed to be candy-less, and TV-less.

But wait. What if there was a way to get that candy without the horrid hassle of learning to spell? Suddenly, Henry had a brilliant, spectacular idea. It was so simple Henry couldn't believe he'd never thought of it before.

He sat next to Clever Clare. Clare always knew the spelling words. All Henry had to do was to take a little peek at her work. If he positioned his chair right, he'd easily be able to see what she wrote. And he wouldn't be copying her, no way. Just double-checking. I am a genius, thought Horrid Henry. 100% right on the test. Loads of Big Bopper candy. Mom and Dad would be so thrilled they'd let him watch extra TV. Hurray!

Horrid Henry swaggered into class the

next morning. He sat down in his seat
between Clever Clare and Beefy Bert.
Carefully, he inched his chair over a
fraction so that he had a good view of
Clare's paper.

"Spelling test!" barked Miss Battle-
Axe. "First word—goat."

Clare bent over her paper. Henry
pretended he was staring at the wall,
then, quick as a flash, he glanced at her
work and wrote "goat."

"Boat," said Miss Battle-Axe.
Again Horrid Henry sneaked a look
at Clare's paper and copied her.
And again. And again.

This is fantastic, thought Henry. I'll
never have to learn any spelling words.
Just think of all the comic books he
could read instead of wasting his time
on homework! He sneaked a peek
at Beefy Bert's paper. Blank. Ha ha,
thought Henry.

There was only one word left.
Henry could taste the tingly tang of
a Big Bopper already. Wouldn't he
swagger around! And no way would he
share his candy with anyone.

Suddenly, Clare shifted position and
edged away from him. Rats! Henry
couldn't see her paper anymore.

"Last word," boomed Miss Battle-
Axe. "Friend."

Henry twisted in his seat. He could
see the first four words. He just needed
to get a tiny bit closer…

Clare looked at him. Henry stared at
the ceiling. Clare glared, then looked

back at her paper. Quickly, Henry
leaned over and...YES! He copied
down the final word, "friend."

Victory!

Chomp! Chomp! Chomp! Mmmmm,
boy, did those Big Boppers taste great!

Someone tapped him on the shoulder.
It was Miss Battle-Axe. She was smiling
at him with her great big yellow teeth.

Miss Battle-Axe had never smiled at Henry before.

"Well, Henry," said Miss Battle-Axe. "What an improvement! I'm thrilled."

"Thank you," said Henry modestly.

"In fact, you've done so well I'm promoting you to the top spelling group. Twenty-five extra words a night. Here's the list."

Horrid Henry's jaws stopped chomping. He looked in horror at the new spelling list. It was littered with words. But not just any words. Awful words. Mean words. Long words. HARD words.

Hieroglyphs.

Trapezium.

Diarrhea.

"AAAAAHHHHHHHHHHH!" shrieked Horrid Henry.

HORRID HENRY'S SCHOOL PROJECT

....

"Susan! Stop shouting!

Ralph! Stop running!

William! Stop weeping!

Henry! Just stop!"

Miss Battle-Axe glared at her class.

Her class glared back.

"Miss!" screeched Lazy Linda.

"Henry's pulling my hair."

"Miss!" screeched Gorgeous Gurinder.

"Ralph's kicking me."

"Miss!" screeched Anxious Andrew.

"Dave's poking me."

"Stop it, Henry!" barked Miss Battle-Axe.

Henry stopped. What was bothering the old bat now?

"Class, pay attention," said Miss Battle-Axe. "Today we're doing Group Projects on the Ancient Greeks. We're studying—"

"—the sacking of Troy!" shrieked Henry. Yes! He could see it now. Henry, leading the Greeks as they crashed and slashed their way through the terrified Trojans. His spear would be the longest, and the sharpest, and—

Miss Battle-Axe fixed Henry with her icy stare. Henry froze.

"We're going to divide into small groups and make Parthenons out of cardboard toilet paper rolls and construction paper," continued Miss Battle-Axe. "First you must draw the Parthenon, agree on a design together, then build and paint it. I want to see *everyone* sharing and listening. "Also, the Principal will be dropping by to admire your work and to see how beautifully you are working together."

Horrid Henry scowled. He hated
working in groups. He detested sharing.
He loathed listening to others. Their
ideas were always wrong. His ideas were
always right. But the other children
in Henry's groups never recognized
Henry's genius. For some reason they
wanted to do things *their* way, not his.

The Ancient Greeks certainly never
worked together beautifully, thought
Horrid Henry resentfully, so why
should he? They just speared each other
or ate their children for dinner.

"Henry, Bert, William, and Clare,
you're working together on Table
Three," said Miss Battle-Axe.

Horrid Henry groaned. What a horrible, horrible group. He hated all of them.
Why didn't Miss Battle-Axe ever put him
in a fun group, with Ralph or Graham or
Dave? Henry could see it now. They'd be
laughing together in the corner, making

trumpets out of toilet paper rolls, sneaking candy, throwing crayons, flicking paint, having a great time.

But oh no. He had to be with bossyboots Clare, crybaby William and—Bert. Miss Battle-Axe did it on purpose, just to torture him.

"NO!" protested Horrid Henry. "I can't work with *her!*"

"NO!" protested Clever Clare. "I can't work with *him!*"

"Waaaaah," wailed Weepy William. "I want to work with Andrew."

"Silence!" shouted Miss Battle-Axe. "Now get in your groups and get to work. I want to see everyone sharing and working together beautifully—or else."

There was a mad scramble as everyone ran to their tables to grab the best pencils and the most pieces of paper.

Henry snatched the purple, blue, and red pencils and a big pile of paper.

"I haven't got any paper!" screamed William.

"Tough," said Horrid Henry. "I need all these for my design."

"I want some paper!" whined William.

Clever Clare passed him one of her sheets.

William burst into tears.

"It's dirty," he wailed. "And I haven't got a pencil."

"Here's what we're going to do," said Henry. "I'm doing the design, William can help me build it, and everyone can watch me paint."

"No way, Henry," said Clare. "We *all* do a design, then we make the best one."

"Which will be mine," said Horrid Henry.

"Doubt it," said Clever Clare.

"Well I'm not making *yours*," snarled Henry. "And *I'm* doing the painting."

"You're doing the gluing, *I'm* doing the painting," said Clare.

"I want to do the painting," wailed William.

"What do you want to do, Bert?" asked Clare.

"I dunno," said Beefy Bert.

"Fine," said Clever Clare. "Bert will do the cleaning. Let's get drawing, everyone. We want our group's Parthenon to be the best."

Horrid Henry was outraged.

"Who made you boss?" demanded Henry.

"Someone has to take charge," said Clever Clare.

Horrid Henry reached under the table and kicked her.

"OOWWWW!" yelped Clever Clare. "Miss! Henry kicked me!"

"Did not!" shouted Horrid Henry. "Liar."

"Why isn't Table Three drawing?" hissed Miss Battle-Axe.

Clare drew.

William drew.

Bert drew.

Henry drew.

"Everyone should have finished drawing by now," said Miss Battle-Axe, patrolling among the tables. "Time to combine your ideas."

"But I haven't finished," wept William.

Horrid Henry gazed at his design with satisfaction. It was a triumph. He could see it now, painted silver and purple, with a few red stripes.

"Why don't we just build mine?" said Clare.

"'Cause mine's the best!" shouted Horrid Henry.

"What about mine?" whispered William.

"We're building mine!" shouted Clare.

"MINE!"

"MINE!"

Miss Battle-Axe ran over.

"Stop shouting!" shouted Miss Battle-Axe. "Show me your work. That's lovely, Clare. What a fabulous design."

"Thank you, Miss," said Clever Clare.

"William! That's a tower, not a temple! Start again!"

"Waaaah!" wailed William.

"Bert! What is this mess?"

"I dunno," said Beefy Bert.

"It looks like a teepee, not a temple," said Miss Battle-Axe.

She looked at Horrid Henry's design and glared at him.

"Can't you follow instructions?" she shrieked. "That temple looks like it's about to blast off."

"That's how I meant it to look," said Henry. "It's high-tech."

"Margaret! Sit down! Toby! Leave Brian alone! Graham! Get back to work," said Miss Battle-Axe, racing off to stop the fight at Table Two.

"Okay, we're doing *my* design," said Clare. "Who wants to build the steps and who wants to decorate the columns?"

"No one," snapped Horrid Henry, "'cause we're doing *mine*."

"Fine, we'll vote," said Clare. "Who wants to build mine?"

Clare and William raised their hands.

"I'll get you for that, William," muttered Henry.

William burst into tears.

"Who wants to do Henry's?" said Clare.

Only Henry raised his hand.

"Come on, Bert, don't you want to make mine?" pleaded Henry.

"I dunno," said Beefy Bert.

"It's not fair!" shrieked Horrid Henry. "I WANT TO BUILD MINE!"

"MINE!"

"MINE!"

SLAP!

SLAP!

"That's it!" shrieked Miss Battle-Axe. "Henry! Work in the corner on your own."

YES! This was the best news Henry had heard all morning.

Beaming, Henry went to the corner and sat down at his own little table, with his own glue, his own scissors, his own paints, his own construction paper, and his own pile of toilet paper rolls.

Bliss, thought Henry. I can build my Parthenon in peace.

There was just one problem. There was only a small number of toilet paper rolls left.

This isn't nearly enough for my Parthenon, thought Horrid Henry. I need more.

He went over to Moody Margaret's table.

"I need more rolls," he said.

"Tough," said Margaret. "We're using all of ours."

Henry stomped over to Sour Susan's table.

"Give me some rolls," he said.

"Go away," said Susan sourly.
"Margaret took our extras."

"Sit down, Henry," barked Miss
Battle-Axe.

Henry sat, fuming. This was an
outrage. Hadn't Miss Battle-Axe
told them to share? And here were
his greedy classmates hogging all the
toilet paper rolls when his Parthenon
desperately needed extra engines.

BUZZZ. Break time!

"Leave your Parthenons on the tables to dry," said Miss Battle-Axe. "Henry, you will stay in at break and finish."

What?

Miss break?

"But—but—"

"Sit down," ordered Miss Battle-Axe. "Or you'll go straight to the Principal's Office!"

Eeeek! Horrid Henry knew the Principal, Mrs. Oddbod, all too well. He did not need to know her any better.

Henry slunk back to his chair. Everyone else ran shrieking out of the door to the playground. Why was it always children who were punished? Why weren't teachers ever sent to the Principal's Office? It was so unfair!

"I just have to run down the hall for a moment. Don't you dare leave that table," said Miss Battle-Axe.

The moment Miss Battle-Axe left the room, Henry jumped up and accidentally on purpose knocked over Clare's chair. He broke William's pencil and drew a skull and crossbones on Bert's teepee.

Then he wandered over to Sour Susan's table. There was a freshly glued Parthenon, waiting to be painted.

Henry studied it.

You know, he thought, Susan's group hasn't done a bad job. Not bad at all. Shame about that bulge on the side, though. If they shared one roll with me, it would balance so much better.

Horrid Henry looked to the left.

He looked to the right.

Snatch! Susan's supports sagged.

Better even that up, thought Horrid Henry.

Yank!

Hmmm, thought Horrid Henry, glancing at Gurinder's table. What were they thinking? Those walls are far too tall.

Grab! Gurinder's temple tottered.

And as for Clare's pathetic efforts, it was positively bursting with useless pillars.

Whisk! Clare's columns wobbled.

Much better, thought Horrid Henry. Soon he had plenty of rolls.

CLOMP

CLOMP

CLOMP

Horrid Henry dashed back to his table and was

innocently gluing away as the class stampeded back to their tables.

Wobble

Wobble

Wobble—CRASH!

On every table, Parthenons started collapsing.

Everyone shrieked and screamed and sobbed.

"It's your fault!"

"Yours!"

"You didn't glue it right!"

"You didn't build it right!"

Rude Ralph hurled a paintbrush at Moody Margaret. Margaret hurled it

back. Suddenly the room was filled with
flying brushes, glue pots, and rolls.

Miss Battle-Axe burst in.

"STOP IT!" bellowed Miss Battle-
Axe, as a roll hit her on the nose.
"YOU ARE THE WORST CLASS
I HAVE EVER TAUGHT! I LEAVE
YOU ALONE FOR ONE MINUTE
AND JUST LOOK AT THIS MESS!
NOW SIT DOWN AND SHUT—"

The door opened. In walked the
principal.

Mrs. Oddbod stared at Miss Battle-Axe.

Miss Battle-Axe stared at Mrs. Oddbod.

"Boudicca!" said Mrs. Oddbod. "What-is-going-on?"

"The sacking of Troy!" shrieked Horrid Henry.

There was a terrible silence.

Horrid Henry shrank in his seat. Now he was done for. Now he was dead.

"I can see that," said Mrs. Oddbod coldly. "Miss Battle-Axe! Come to my office—now!"

"No!" whimpered Miss Battle-Axe.

YES! thought Horrid Henry.

Victory!

HORRID HENRY
READS A BOOK

Blah blah blah blah blah.

Miss Battle-Axe droned on and on and on. Horrid Henry drew pictures of crocodiles munching on a juicy Battle-Axe snack in his math book.

Snap! Off went her head.

Yank! Bye-bye leg.

Crunch! Ta-ta teeth.

Yum yum. Henry's crocodile had a big fat smile on its face.

Blah blah blah books blah blah blah read blah blah blah prize blah blah

…PRIZE?

Horrid Henry stopped doodling.

"What prize?" he shrieked.

"Don't shout out, Henry," said Miss Battle-Axe.

Horrid Henry waved his hand and shouted:

"What prize?"

"Well, Henry, if you'd been paying attention instead of scribbling, you'd know, wouldn't you?" said Miss Battle-Axe.

Horrid Henry scowled. Typical teacher. You're interested enough in what they're saying to ask a question, and suddenly they don't want to answer.

"So, class, as I was saying before I was so rudely interrupted—" she glared at Horrid Henry— "you'll have two weeks to read as many books as you can for our school reading competition. Whoever reads the most books will win an exciting prize. A very exciting prize. But remember, a book report on every book on your list, please."

Oh. A reading competition. Horrid Henry slumped in his chair. Phooey. Reading was hard, heavy work. Just turning the pages made Henry feel exhausted. Why couldn't they ever do fun competitions, like whose tummy could rumble the loudest, or who shouted out the most in class, or who knew the rudest words? Horrid Henry would win *those* competitions every time.

But no. Miss Battle-Axe would never have a *fun* competition. Well, no way was he taking part in a reading contest.

Henry would just have to watch someone undeserving like Clever Clare or Brainy Brian swagger off with the prize while he sat prize-less at the back. It was so unfair!

"What's the prize?" shouted Moody Margaret.

Probably something awful like a pencil case, thought Horrid Henry. Or a bumper pack of school dish rags.

"Candy!" shouted Greedy Graham.

"A million bucks!" shouted Rude Ralph.

"Clothes!" shouted Gorgeous Gurinder.

"A skateboard!" shouted Aerobic Al.

"A hamster!" said Anxious Andrew.

"Silence!" bellowed Miss Battle-Axe. "The prize is a family ticket to a brand new theme park."

Horrid Henry sat up. A theme park! Oh wow! He loved theme parks! Roller coasters! Water rides! Cotton candy! His mean, horrible parents never took him

to theme parks. They dragged him to
museums. They hauled him on hikes. But
if he won the competition, they'd have to
take him. He had to win that prize. He
had to. But how could he win a reading
competition without reading any books?

"Do comics count?" shouted Rude
Ralph.

Horrid Henry's heart leapt.
He was king of the
comic book readers.
He'd easily win a comic
book competition.

Miss Battle-Axe
glared at Ralph with
her beady eyes.

"Of course not!"
she said. "Clare! How
many books do you
think you can read?"

"Fifteen," said Clever
Clare.

"Brian?"

"Eighteen," said Brainy Brian.

"Nineteen," said Clare.

"Twenty," said Brian.

Horrid Henry smiled. Wouldn't they get a shock when *he* won the prize? He'd start reading the second he got home.

Horrid Henry stretched out in the comfy black chair and switched on the TV. He had plenty of time to read. He'd start tomorrow.

Tuesday. Oh boy! Five new comics!

He'd read them first and start on all
those books later.

Wednesday. Whoopee! A *Mutant
Max* TV special! He'd definitely get
reading afterward.

Thursday. Rude Ralph brought over
his great new computer game, "Mash
'em! Smash 'em!" Henry mashed and
smashed and mashed and smashed…

Friday. Yawn. Horrid Henry was
exhausted after his long, hard week. I'll
read tons of books tomorrow, thought
Henry. After all, there was tons of time
till the competition ended.

"How many books have *you* read,
Henry?" asked Perfect Peter, looking up
from the sofa.

"Tons," lied Henry.

"I've read five," said Perfect Peter
proudly. "More than anyone in my
class."

"Goody for you," said Henry.

"You're just jealous," said Peter.

"As if I'd ever be jealous of you, worm," sneered Henry. He wandered over to the sofa. "So what are you reading?"

"*The Happy Nappy*," said Peter.

The Happy Nappy! Trust Peter to read a stupid book like that.

"What's it about?" asked Henry, snorting.

"It's great," said Peter. "It's all about this diaper—" Then he stopped. "Wait, I'm not telling *you*. You just want to find out so you can use it in the competition. Well, you're too late. Tomorrow is the last day."

Horrid Henry felt as if a dagger had been plunged into his heart. This couldn't be. Tomorrow! How had tomorrow sneaked up so fast?

"What!" shrieked Henry. "The competition ends—tomorrow?"

"Yes," said Peter. "You should have

started reading sooner. After all, why put off till tomorrow what you can do today?"

"Shut up!" said Horrid Henry. He looked around wildly. What to do, what to do. He had to read something, anything—fast.

"Gimme that!" snarled Henry, snatching Peter's book. Frantically, he started to read:

"I'm unhappy, pappy," said the snappy nappy. "A happy nappy is a clappy—"

Perfect Peter snatched back his book.

"No!" screamed Peter, holding on tightly. "It's mine."

Henry lunged.

"Mine!"

"Mine!"

Riii—iippp.

"MOOOOMMMM!" screamed Peter. "Henry tore my book!"

Mom and Dad ran into the room.

"You're fighting—over a book?" said Mom. She sat down in a chair.

"I'm speechless," said Mom.

"Well, I'm not," said Dad. "Henry! Go to your room!"

"Fine!" screamed Horrid Henry.

Horrid Henry prowled up and down his bedroom. He had to think of something. Fast.

Aha! The room was full of books. He'd just copy down lots of titles. Phew. Easy-peasy.

And then suddenly Horrid Henry remembered. He had to write a book

report for every book he read. Rats.
Miss Battle-Axe knew tons and tons of
books. She was sure to know the plot
of *Jack the Kangaroo* or *The Adventures of
Terry the Towel.*

Well, he'd just have to borrow Peter's
list.

Horrid Henry sneaked into Peter's
bedroom. There was Peter's competition
entry, in the center of Peter's immacu-
late desk. Henry read it.

Of course Peter would have the boring
and horrible *Mouse Goes to Town.* Could
he live with the shame of having baby
books like *The Happy Nappy* and *Mouse
Goes to Town* on his competition entry?

For a day at a theme park, anything.

Quickly, Henry copied Peter's list and book reports. Whoopee! Now he had five books. Wheel of Death here I come, thought Horrid Henry.

Then Henry had to face the terrible truth. Peter's books wouldn't be enough to win. He'd heard Clever Clare had seventeen. If only he didn't have to write those book reports. Why, oh why, did Miss Battle-Axe have to know every book ever written?

And then suddenly Henry had a brilliant, spectacular idea. It was so brilliant, and so simple, that Horrid Henry was amazed. Of course there were books that Miss Battle-Axe didn't know. Books that hadn't been written—yet.

Horrid Henry grabbed his list.

"*Mouse Goes to Town*. The thrilling adventures of a mouse in town. He meets a dog, a cat, and a duck."

Why should that poor mouse just go to town? Quickly Henry began to scribble.

"*Mouse Goes to the Country*. The thrilling adventures of a mouse in the country. He meets—"

Henry paused. What sort of things *did* you meet in the country? Henry had no idea.

Aha. Henry wrote quickly. "He meets a sheep and a werewolf."

"*Mouse Goes Around the World*. Mouse discovers that the world is round."

"*Mouse Goes to the Bathroom*. The thrilling adventures of one mouse and his potty."

Now, perhaps, something a little different. How about *A Boy and his Pig*. What could that book be about? thought Henry.

"Once upon a time there was a boy and his pig. They played together every day. The pig went oink."

Sounds good to me, thought Henry.

Then there was *A Pig and his Boy*. And, of course, *A Boyish Pig*. *A Piggish Boy*. *Two Pigs and a Boy*. *Two Boys and a Pig*.

Horrid Henry wrote and wrote and wrote. When he had filled up four pages with books and reports, and his hand ached from writing, he stopped and counted.

Twenty-seven books! Surely that was more than enough!

Miss Battle-Axe rose from her seat and walked to the podium in the school hall. Horrid Henry was so excited he could scarcely breathe. He had to win. He was sure to win.

"Well done, everyone," said Miss Battle-Axe. "So many wonderful books read. But sadly, there can be only one winner."

Me! thought Horrid Henry.

"The winner of the school reading competition, the winner who will be receiving a fabulous prize, is—" Horrid

Henry got ready to leap up— "Clare, with twenty-eight books!"

Horrid Henry sank back down in his seat as Clever Clare swaggered up to the podium. If only he'd added *Three Boys, Two Pigs, and a Rhinoceros* to his list, he'd have tied for first. It was so unfair. All his hard work for nothing.

"Well done, Clare!" beamed Miss Battle-Axe. She waved Clare's list. "I see you've read one of my very favorites, *Boudicca's Big Battle*."

She stopped. "Oh dear. Clare, you've put down *Boudicca's Big Battle* twice by mistake. But never mind. I'm sure no one else has read *twenty-seven* books—"

"I have!" screamed Horrid Henry. Leaping and shouting, punching the air with his fist, Horrid Henry ran up onto the stage, chanting: "Theme park! Theme park! Theme park!"

"Gimme my prize!" he screeched, snatching the tickets out of Clare's hand.

"Mine!" screamed Clare, snatching them back.

Miss Battle-Axe looked grim. She scanned Henry's list.

"I am not familiar with the *Boy and Pig* series," she said.

"That's 'cause it's Australian," said Horrid Henry.

Miss Battle-Axe glared at him. Then she tried to twist her face into a smile.

"It appears we have a tie," she said. "Therefore, you will each receive a family pass to the new theme park, Book World. Congratulations."

Horrid Henry stopped his victory dance. Book World? Book World? Surely he'd heard wrong?

"Here are just some of the wonderful attractions you will enjoy at Book World," said Miss Battle-Axe. "'Thrill to a display of speed-reading! Practice checking out library books! Read to the beat!' Oh my, doesn't that sound fun!"

"AAAAAARGGGGGGGGG!" screamed Horrid Henry.

HORRID HENRY'S UNDERPANTS

....

A late birthday present! Whoopee! Just when you thought you'd got all your loot, more treasure arrives.

Horrid Henry shook the small thin package. It was light. Very light. Maybe it was—oh, please let it be—MONEY! Of course it was money. What else could it be? There was so much stuff he needed: a *Mutant Max* lunch box, a Rapper Zapper Blaster, and, of course, the new *Terminator Gladiator* game he kept seeing advertised on TV. Mom and Dad were so mean and horrible, they wouldn't buy it for him. But he could buy whatever he liked with his

own money. So there. Ha ha ha ha ha.
Wouldn't Ralph be green with envy
when he swaggered into school with
a Mutant Max lunch box? And no
way would he even let Peter touch his
Rapper Zapper Blaster.

So how much money had he been
sent? Maybe enough for him to buy
everything! Horrid Henry tore off the
wrapping paper.

AAAAARRRRGGGHHHHH!
Great-Aunt Greta had done it again.

Great-Aunt Greta thought he was a
girl. Great-Aunt Greta had been told ten
billion times that his name was Henry,
not Henrietta, and that he wasn't four
years old. But every year Peter would get
$10, or a football, or a computer game,
and he would get a Walkie-Talkie-
Teasy-Weasy-Burpy-Slurpy Doll. Or a
Princess Pamper Parlor. Or Baby Poopie
Pants. And now this.

Horrid Henry picked up the birthday card. Maybe there was money inside. He opened it.

> Dear Henry,
> You must be such a big girl now, so I know you'd love a pair of big girl underpants. I'll bet pink is your favorite color.
> Love, Great-Aunt Greta

Horrid Henry stared in horror at the frilly pink lacy underpants, decorated with glittery hearts and bows. This was the worst present he had ever received. Worse than socks. Worse than handkerchiefs. Even worse than a book.

Bleccch! Ick! Yuck! Horrid Henry chucked the hideous underpants in the garbage where they belonged.

Ding dong.

Oh no! Rude Ralph was here to play. If he saw those underpants Henry would never hear the end of it. His name would be mud forever.

Clump clump clump.

Ralph was stomping up the stairs to his bedroom. Henry snatched the terrible underpants from the garbage and looked around his room wildly for a hiding place. Under the pillow? What if they had a pillow fight? Under the bed? What if they played hide and seek? Quickly Henry stuffed them in the back of his underpants drawer. I'll get rid of them the moment Ralph leaves, he thought.

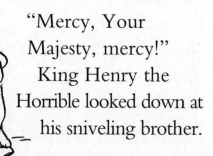

"Mercy, Your Majesty, mercy!" King Henry the Horrible looked down at his sniveling brother.

"Off with his head!" he ordered.

"Henry! Henry! Henry!" cheered his grateful subjects.

"HENRY!"

King Henry the Horrible woke up. His Medusa mother was looming above him.

"You've overslept!" shrieked Mom. "School starts in five minutes! Get dressed! Quick! Quick!" She pulled the blanket off Henry.

"Wha—wha?" mumbled Henry.

Dad raced into the room.

"Hurry!" shouted Dad. "We're late!" He yanked Henry out of bed.

Henry stumbled around his dark bedroom. Half-asleep, he reached inside his underwear drawer, grabbed a pair, then picked up some clothes off the floor and flung everything on. Then he, Dad, and Peter ran all the way to school.

"Margaret! Stop pulling Susan's hair!"

"Ralph! Sit down!"

"Linda! Sit up!"

"Henry! Pay attention!" barked Miss Battle-Axe. "I am about to explain long division. I will only explain it once. You take a great big number, like 374, and then divide it—"

Horrid Henry was not paying attention. He was tired. He was crabby. And for some reason his underpants were itchy.

These underpants feel horrible, he thought. And so tight. What's wrong with them?

Horrid Henry sneaked a peek.

94

And then
Horrid Henry saw
what underpants he
had on. Not
his Driller Cannibal
underpants. Not his
Marvin the Maniac
ones either. Not
even his old Gross-Out ones, with the
holes and the droopy elastic.

He, Horrid Henry, was wearing frilly
pink lacy girls' underpants covered in
glittery hearts and bows. He'd completely
forgotten he'd stuffed them into his
underpants drawer last month so Ralph
wouldn't see them. And now, oh horror
of horrors, he was wearing them.

Maybe it's a nightmare, thought
Horrid Henry hopefully. He pinched
his arm. Ouch! Then, just to be sure, he
pinched William.

"Waaaaah!" wailed Weepy William.

"Stop weeping, William!" said Miss Battle-Axe. "Now, what number do I need—"

It was not a nightmare. He was still in school, still wearing pink underpants.

What to do, what to do?

Don't panic, thought Horrid Henry. He took a deep breath. Don't panic. After all, no one will know. His pants weren't see-through or anything.

Wait. What pants was he wearing? Were there any holes in them? Quickly Horrid Henry twisted round to check his bottom.

Phew. There were no holes. What luck he hadn't put on his old jeans with the big rip but a new pair.

He was safe.

"Henry! What's the answer?" said Miss Battle-Axe.

"Pants," said Horrid Henry before he could stop himself.

The class burst out laughing.

"Pants!" screeched Rude Ralph.

"Pants!" screeched Dizzy Dave.

"Henry. Stand up," ordered Miss Battle-Axe.

Henry stood. His heart was pounding. Slip!

Aaaarrrghhh! The lacy ruffle of his pink underpants was showing! His new pants were too big. Mom always bought him clothes that were way too big so he'd grow into them. These were the falling-down ones he'd tried on yesterday. Henry gripped his pants tight and yanked them up.

"What did you say?" said Miss Battle-Axe slowly.

"Ants," said Horrid Henry.

"Ants?" said Miss Battle-Axe.

"Yeah," said Henry quickly. "I was just thinking about how many ants you could divide by—by that number you said," he added.

Miss Battle-Axe glared at him.

"I've got my eye on you, Henry," she snapped. "Now sit down and pay attention."

Henry sat. All he had to do was tuck in his T-shirt. That would keep his pants up. He'd look stupid but for once Henry didn't care.

Just so long as no one ever knew about his pink lacy underpants.

And then Henry's blood turned to ice. What was the latest craze on the playground? Depantsing. Who'd started it? Horrid Henry. Yesterday he'd chased Dizzy

Dave and pulled down his pants. The day before he'd done the same thing to Rude Ralph. Just this morning he'd depantsed Tough Toby on the way into class.

They'd all be trying to depants him now.

I have to get another pair of underpants, thought Henry desperately.

Miss Battle-Axe passed around the math worksheets. Quickly Horrid Henry scribbled down: 3, 7, 41, 174, without reading any questions. He didn't have time for long division.

Where could he find some other underpants? He could pretend to be sick and get sent home from school. But he'd already tried that twice this week. Wait. Wait. He was brilliant. He was a genius. What about the Lost and Found? Someone, some time, must have lost some underpants.

DING! DING!

Before the playtime bell had finished ringing Horrid Henry was out of his seat and racing down the hall, holding tight to his pants. He checked carefully to make sure no one was watching, then ducked into the Lost and Found. He'd hide here until he found some underpants.

The Lost and Found was stuffed with clothes. He rummaged through the mountains of lost shoes, socks, jackets, pants, shirts, coats, lunch boxes, hats, and gloves. I'm amazed anyone leaves school wearing *anything*, thought Horrid

Henry, tossing another sweatshirt over
his shoulder.

Then—hurray! Underpants. A pair of
blue underpants. What a wonderful sight.

Horrid Henry pulled the underpants
from the pile. Oh no. They were the
teeniest, tiniest pair he'd ever seen.
Some toddler must have lost them.

Rats, thought Horrid Henry. Well,
no way was he wearing his horrible
pink underpants a second longer. He'd
just have to trade underpants with
someone. And Horrid Henry had the
perfect someone in mind.

Henry found Peter in the playground playing tag with Tidy Ted.

"I need to talk to you in private," said Henry. "It's urgent."

"What about?" said Peter cautiously.

"It's top secret," said Henry. Out of the corner of his eye he saw Dave and Toby sneaking toward him.

Top secret! Henry never shared top secret secrets with Peter.

"Quick!" yelped Henry. "There's no time to lose!"

He ducked into the boys' bathroom. Peter followed.

"Peter, I'm worried about you," said Horrid Henry. He tried to look concerned.

"I'm fine," said Peter.

"No you're not," said Henry. "I've heard bad things about you."

"What bad things?" said Peter anxiously. Not—not that he had run across the carpet in class?

"Embarrassing rumors," said Horrid
Henry. "But if I don't tell you, who
will? After all," he said, putting his arm
around Peter's shoulder, "it's my job to
look after you. Big brothers should look
out for little ones."

Perfect Peter could not believe his
ears.

"Oh, Henry," said Peter. "I've always
wanted a brother who looked out for me."

"That's me," said Henry. "Now listen.
I've heard you wear baby underpants."

"I do not," said Peter. "Look!" And

he showed Henry his Daffy and her Dancing Daisies underpants.

Horrid Henry's heart went cold. Daffy and her Dancing Daisies! Ugh. Yuck. Gross. But even Daffy would be a million billion times better than pink underpants with lace ruffles.

"Daffy Daisy are the most babyish underpants you could wear," said Henry. "Worse than wearing a diaper. Everyone will tease you."

Peter's lip trembled. He hated being teased.

"What can I do?" he asked.

Henry pretended to think. "Look. I'll do you a big favor. I'll swap my underpants for yours. That way I'll get teased, not you."

"Thank you, Henry," said Peter. "You're the best brother in the world." Then he stopped.

"Wait a minute," he said suspiciously, "let's see your underpants."

"Why?" said Henry.

"Because," said Peter, "how do I know you've even got underpants to swap?"

Horrid Henry was outraged.

"Of course I've got underpants," said Henry.

"Then show me," said Peter.

Horrid Henry was trapped.

"OK," he said, giving Peter a quick flash of pink lace.

Perfect Peter stared at Henry's underpants.

"Those are your underpants?" he said.

"Sure," said Horrid Henry. "These are big boy underpants."

"But they're pink," said Peter.

"All big boys wear pink," said Henry.

"But they have lace on them," said Peter.

"All big boys' pants have lace," said Henry.

"But they have hearts and bows," said Peter.

"Of course they do, they're big boy underpants," said Horrid Henry. "You wouldn't know because you only wear baby underpants."

Peter hesitated.

"But...but...they look like—girls' underpants," said Peter.

Henry snorted. "Girls' underpants! Do you think I'd ever wear girls' underpants? These are what all the big kids are wearing. You'll be the coolest kid in class in these."

Perfect Peter backed away.

"No I won't," said Peter.

"Yes you will," said Henry.

"I don't want to wear your smelly underpants," said Peter.

"They're not smelly," said Henry. "They're brand new. Now give me your underpants."

"NO!" screamed Peter.

"YES!" screamed Henry. "Give me your underpants!"

"What's going on in here?" came a voice of steel. It was the principal, Mrs. Oddbod.

"Nothing," said Henry.

"There's no hanging around the bathroom at playtime," said Mrs. Oddbod. "Out of here, both of you."

Peter ran out the door.

Now what do I do, thought Horrid Henry.

Henry ducked into a stall and hid the pink underpants on the ledge above the third toilet. No way was he putting those underpants back on. Better Henry No Underpants than Henry Pink Underpants.

★ ★ ★

At lunchtime Horrid Henry dodged
Graham. He dodged Toby by the
climbing frame. During last play Dave
almost caught him by the water
fountain but Henry was too quick.
Ralph chased him into class but Henry
got to his seat just in time. He'd done
it! Only forty-five minutes to go until
home time. There'd be no depantsing
after school with parents around.
Henry couldn't believe it. He was safe
at last.

He stuck out his tongue at Ralph.

"Nah nah ne nah ne," he jeered.

Miss Battle-Axe clapped her claws.

"Time to change for P.E." said Miss
Battle-Axe.

P.E.! It couldn't be—not a P.E. day.

"And I don't care if aliens stole your
P.E. uniform, Henry," said Miss Battle-
Axe, glaring at him. "No excuses."

That's what she thought. He had the

perfect excuse. Even a teacher as mean and horrible as Miss Battle-Axe would not force a boy to do P.E. without underpants.

Horrid Henry went up to Miss Battle-Axe and whispered in her ear.

"Forgot your underpants, eh?" barked Miss Battle-Axe loudly.

Henry blushed scarlet. When he was king he'd make Miss Battle-Axe walk around town every  day wearing underpants on her head.

"Well, Henry, today is your lucky day," said Miss Battle-Axe, pulling something pink and lacy out of her pocket. "I found these in the boys' bathroom."

"Take them away!" screamed Horrid Henry.

HORRID HENRY'S AUTHOR VISIT

·····························

Horrid Henry woke up. He felt strange. He felt…happy. He felt…excited. But why?

Was it the weekend? No. Was it a day off school? No. Had Miss Battle-Axe been kidnapped by aliens and transported to another galaxy to slave in the salt mines? No (unfortunately).

So why was he feeling so excited on a school day?

And then Horrid Henry remembered.

Oh wow!! It was Book Week at Henry's school, and his favorite author in the whole world, TJ Fizz, the writer

of the stupendous *Ghost Quest* and
Mad Machines and *Skeleton Skunks*, was
coming to talk to his class. Henry had
read every single one of TJ's brilliant
books, even after lights out. Rude
Ralph thought they were almost as good
as *Mutant Max* comics. Horrid Henry
thought they were even better.

Perfect Peter bounced into his room.

"Isn't it exciting, Henry?" said Perfect
Peter. "Our class is going to meet a real live
author! Milksop Miles is coming today.
He's the man who wrote *The Happy
Nappy*. Do you think he'll sign my copy?"

Horrid Henry snorted.

The Happy Nappy! Only the
dumbest book ever. All those giant
diapers with names like
Rappy Nappy and Zappy
Nappy and Tappy Nappy
dancing and prancing around.
And then the truly

horrible Gappy Nappy, who was always
wailing, "I'm leaking!"

Horrid Henry shuddered. He was
amazed that Milksop Miles dared to
show his face after writing such a
boring book.

"Only a wormy toad like you could
like such a stupid story," said Henry.

"It's not stupid," said Peter.

"Is too."

"Is not. And he's bringing his guitar.
Miss Lovely said so."

"Big deal," said Horrid Henry. "*We've*
got TJ Fizz."

Perfect Peter shuddered.

"Her books are too scary," said Peter.

"That's 'cause you're a baby."

"Mom!" shrieked Peter. "Henry called me a baby."

"Tattletale," hissed Henry.

"Don't be horrid, Henry," shouted Mom.

Horrid Henry sat in class with a huge tote bag filled with all his TJ Fizz books. Everyone in the class had drawn book covers for *Ghost Quest* and *Ghouls' Jewels,* and written their own *Skeleton Skunk* story. Henry's of course was the best: *Skeleton Skunk Meets*

Terminator Gladiator: May the Smelliest Fighter Win! He would give it to TJ Fizz if she paid him a million dollars.

Ten minutes to go. How could he live until it was time for her to arrive?

Miss Battle-Axe cleared her throat.

"Class, we have a very important guest coming. I know you're all very excited, but I will not tolerate anything but perfect behavior today. Anyone who misbehaves will be sent out. Is that clear?" She glared at Henry.

Henry scowled back. Of course he would be perfect. TJ Fizz was coming!

"Has everyone thought of a good question to ask her? I'll write the best ones on the board," continued Miss Battle-Axe.

"How much money do you make?" shouted Rude Ralph.

"How many TVs do you have?" shouted Horrid Henry.

"Do you like fudge?" shouted Greedy Graham.

"I said *good* questions," snapped Miss Battle-Axe. "Bert, what's your question for TJ Fizz?"

"I dunno," said Beefy Bert.

Rumble.

Rumble.

Rumble

Ooops. Henry's tummy was telling him it was snack time.

It must be all the excitement. It was strictly forbidden to eat in class, but Henry was a master sneaker. He certainly wouldn't want his tummy to gurgle while TJ Fizz was talking.

Miss Battle-Axe was writing down Clever Clare's eight questions on the board.

Slowly, carefully, silently, Horrid Henry opened his lunch box under the table. Slowly, carefully, silently, he eased open the bag of chips.

Horrid Henry looked to the left.

Rude Ralph was waving his hand in
the air.

Horrid Henry looked to the right.

Greedy Graham was drooling and
opening a bag of candy.

The coast was clear. Henry popped
some Super Spicy Hedgehog chips into
his mouth.

MUNCH! CRUNCH!

"C'mon Henry, give me some chips,"
whispered Rude Ralph.

"No," hissed Horrid Henry. "Eat your
own."

"I'm starving," moaned Greedy
Graham. "Gimme a chip."

"No!" hissed Horrid Henry.

MUNCH! CRUNCH! YANK

Huh?

Miss Battle-Axe towered over him, holding his bag of chips in the air. Her red eyes were like two icy daggers.

"What did I tell you, Henry?" said Miss Battle-Axe. "No bad behavior would be tolerated. Go to Miss Lovely's class."

"But…but…TJ Fizz is coming!" spluttered Horrid Henry. "I was just—"

Miss Battle-Axe pointed to the door. "Out!"

"NOOOOOOOOOO!" howled Henry.

Horrid Henry sat in a tiny chair at the back of Miss Lovely's room. Never had he suffered such torment. He tried to block his ears as Milksop Miles read his horrible book to Peter's class.

"Hello, Happy, Clappy, and Yappy! Can *you* find the leak?"

"No," said Happy.

"No," said Clappy.

"No," said Yappy.

"I can," said Gappy Nappy.

AAAARRRRGGGGGHHH! Horrid Henry gritted his teeth. He would go crazy having to listen to this a moment longer.

He had to get out of here.

"All together now, let's sing the 'Happy Nappy Song,'" trilled Milksop Miles, whipping out his guitar.

"Yay!" cheered the infants.

No, groaned Horrid Henry.

Oh I'm a happy nappy,
a happy zappy nappy
I wrap up your bottom, snug and tight,
And keep you dry all through the night
Oh—

This was torture. No, this was worse than torture. How could he sit here listening to the horrible "Happy Nappy

121

Song" knowing that just above him TJ Fizz was reading from one of her incredible books, passing around the famous skunk skeleton, and showing off her *Ghost Quest* drawings? He had to get back to his own class. He had to.

But how?

What if he joined in the singing? He could bellow:

> Oh I'm a soggy nappy
> A smelly, stinky nappy—

Yes! That would certainly get him sent out the door straight to—the principal. Not back to his class and TJ Fizz.

Horrid Henry closed his mouth. Rats.

Maybe there'd be an earthquake? A power failure? Where was a fire drill when you needed one?

He could always pretend he needed to use the restroom. But then when he didn't come back, they'd come looking for him.

Or maybe he could just sneak away? Why not? Henry got to his feet and began to slide toward the door, trying to be invisible.

Sneak Sneak Sn—

"Whooa, come back here, little boy," shouted Milksop Miles, twanging his guitar. Henry froze. "Our party is just starting. Now who knows the Happy Nappy Dance?"

"I do," said Perfect Peter.

"I do," said Goody-Goody Gordon.

"We all do," said Tidy Ted.

"Everyone on their feet," said Milksop Miles. "Ah-one, ah-two, let's all do the Nappy Dance!"

"Nap nap nap nap nap nap nappy," warbled Miles.

"Nap nap nap nap nap nap nappy," warbled Peter's class, dancing away.

Desperate times call for desperate

measures. Horrid Henry started dancing. Slowly, he tapped his way closer and closer and closer to the door and—freedom!

Horrid Henry reached for the door knob. Miss Lovely was busy dancing in the corner. Just a few more steps…

"Who's going to be my little helper while we act out the story?" beamed Miles. "Who would like to play the Happy Nappy?"

"Me! Me!" squealed Miss Lovely's class.

Horrid Henry sank against the wall.

"Come on, don't be shy," said Miles, pointing straight at Henry. "Come on up and put on the magic happy nappy!" And he marched over and dangled an enormous blue diaper in front of Henry. It was over one yard wide and one yard high, with a hideous smiling face and big goggly eyes.

Horrid Henry took a step back. He

felt faint. The giant diaper was looming above him. In a moment it would be over his head and he'd be trapped inside. His name would be mud—forever. Henry the nappy. Henry the giant nappy. Henry the giant happy nappy…

"**AAAARRRRGGGGGHHH!**" screamed Horrid Henry. "Get away from me!"

Milksop Miles stopped waving the gigantic diaper.

"Oh dear," he said.

"Oh dear," said Miss Lovely.

"Don't be scared," said Miles.

125

Scared? Horrid Henry…scared? Of a giant diaper? Henry opened his mouth to scream.

And then he stopped.

What if…?

"Help! Help! I'm being attacked by a diaper!" screeched Henry. "HELLLLLLLP!"

Milksop Miles looked at Miss Lovely. Miss Lovely looked at Milksop Miles.

"HELLLLLLLP! HELLLLLLLP!"

"Henry? Are you OK?" piped Perfect Peter.

"NOOOOOOOOO!" wailed Horrid Henry, cowering. "I'm…I'm…diaper-phobic."

"Never mind," said Milksop Miles. "You're not the first boy who's been scared of a giant diaper."

"I'm sure I'll be fine if I go back to my own class," gasped Horrid Henry.

Miss Lovely hesitated. Horrid Henry opened his mouth to howl—

"Run along then," said Miss Lovely quickly.

Horrid Henry did not wait to be told twice.

He raced out of Miss Lovely's class, then dashed upstairs to his own.

Skeleton Skunk here I come, thought Henry, bursting through the door.

There was the great and glorious TJ

Fizz, just about to start reading a brand new chapter from her latest book, *Skeleton Stinkbomb*. Hallelujah, he was in time.

"Henry, what are you doing here?" hissed Miss Battle-Axe.

"Miss Lovely sent me back," beamed Horrid Henry. "And you did say we should be on our best behavior today, so I did what I was told."

Henry sat down as TJ began to read. The story was amazing.

Ahhh, sighed Horrid Henry happily, wasn't life grand?

HORRID HENRY'S DANCE CLASS

....

Stomp Stomp Stomp Stomp Stomp Stomp Stomp.

Horrid Henry was practicing his elephant dance.

Tap Tap Tap Tap Tap Tap Tap Tap.

Perfect Peter was practicing his raindrop dance.

Peter was practicing being a raindrop for his dance class show.

Henry was also supposed to be practicing being a raindrop.

But Henry did not want to be a raindrop. He did not want to be a tomato, a string bean, or a banana either.

Stomp Stomp Stomp went Henry's heavy boots.

Tap Tap Tap went Peter's tap shoes.

"You're doing it wrong, Henry," said Peter.

"No I'm not," said Henry.

"You are too," said Peter. "We're supposed to be raindrops."

Stomp Stomp Stomp went Henry's boots. He was an elephant smashing his way through the jungle, trampling on everyone who stood in his way.

"I can't concentrate with you stomping," said Peter. "And I have to practice my solo."

"Who cares?" screamed Horrid Henry. "I hate dancing, I hate dance class, and most of all, I hate you!"

This was not entirely true. Horrid Henry loved dancing. Henry danced in his bedroom. Henry danced up and down the stairs. Henry danced on the new sofa and on the kitchen table.

What Henry hated was having to dance with other children.

"Couldn't I go to karate instead?" asked Henry every Saturday.

"No," said Mom. "Too violent."

"Judo?" said Henry.

"N–O spells no," said Dad.

So every Saturday morning at 9:45
a.m., Henry and Peter's father drove
them to Miss Impatience Tutu's
Dance Studio.

Miss Impatience
Tutu was skinny
and bony. She had
long stringy gray
hair. Her nose was
sharp. Her elbows
were pointy. Her
knees were knobbly.
No one had ever
seen her smile.

Perhaps this was
because Impatience
Tutu hated teaching.

Impatience Tutu
hated noise.

Impatience Tutu
hated children.

But most of all
Impatience Tutu
hated Horrid Henry.

This was not surprising. When Miss

Tutu shouted, "Class, lift your left legs," eleven left legs lifted. One right leg sagged to the floor.

When Miss Tutu screamed, "Heel, toe, heel, toe," eleven dainty feet tapped away. One clumpy foot stomped toe, heel, toe, heel.

When Miss Tutu bellowed, "Class, skip to your right," eleven bodies turned to the right. One body galumphed to the left.

Naturally, no one wanted to dance with Henry. Or indeed, anywhere near Henry. Today's class, unfortunately, was no different.

"Miss Tutu, Henry is treading on my toes," said Jumpy Jeffrey.

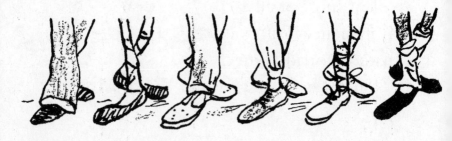

"Miss Tutu, Henry is kicking my legs," said Lazy Linda.

"Miss Tutu, Henry is bumping me," said Vain Violet.

"HENRY!" screeched Miss Tutu.

"Yeah," said Henry.

"I am a patient woman, and you are trying my patience to the limit," hissed Miss Tutu. "Any more bad behavior and you will be very sorry."

"What will happen?" asked Horrid Henry eagerly.

Miss Tutu stood very tall. She took a long, bony finger and dragged it slowly across her throat.

Henry decided that he would
rather live to do battle another day.
He stood on the side, gnashing his
teeth, pretending he was an enormous
crocodile about to gobble up
Miss Tutu.

"This is our final rehearsal before
the show," barked Miss Tutu.
"Everything must be perfect."

Eleven faces stared at Miss Tutu.
One face scowled at the floor.

"Tomatoes and beans to the front,"
ordered Miss Tutu.

"When Miss Thumper plays the
music everyone will stretch out their
arms to the sky to kiss the morning
hello. Raindrops, stand at the back
next to the giant green leaves and
wait until the beans find the magic
bananas. And Henry," spat Miss
Tutu, glaring. "TRY to get it right."

"Positions, everybody. Miss Thumper, the opening music please!" shouted Miss Tutu.

Miss Thumper banged away.

The tomatoes weaved in and out, twirling.

The beans pirouetted.

The bananas pointed their toes and swayed.

The raindrops pitter-patted.

All except one. Henry waved his
arms frantically and raced around
the room. Then he crashed into
the beans.

"HENRY!" screeched Miss Tutu.

"Yeah," scowled Henry.

"Sit in the corner!"

Henry was delighted. He sat in the
corner and made horrible rude faces
while Peter did his raindrop solo.

Tap tap tap tap tap tap tap. Tappa
tappa tappa tappa tap tap tap. Tappa
tip tappa tip tappa tappa tappa tip.

"Was that perfect, Miss Tutu?"
asked Peter.

Miss Tutu sighed. "Perfect, Peter,
as always," she said, and the corner
of her mouth trembled slightly. This
was the closest Miss Tutu ever came
to smiling.

Then she saw Henry slouching on

the chair. Her mouth drooped back into its normal grim position.

Miss Tutu tugged Henry off the chair. She shoved him to the very back of the stage, behind the other raindrops. Then she pushed him behind a giant green leaf.

"Stand there!" shouted Miss Tutu.

"But no one will see me here," said Henry.

"Precisely," said Miss Tutu.

It was showtime.

The curtain was about to rise.

The children stood quietly on stage.

Perfect Peter was so excited he almost bounced up and down. Naturally he controlled himself and stood still.

Horrid Henry was not very
excited.

He did not want to be a raindrop.
And he certainly did not want to be
a raindrop who danced behind a giant
green leaf.

Miss Thumper waddled over to the
piano. She banged on the keys.

The curtain went up.

Henry's mom and dad were in the audience with the other parents. As usual they sat in the back row in case they had to make a quick getaway.

They smiled and waved at Peter standing proudly at the front.

"Can you see Henry?" whispered Henry's mom.

Henry's dad squinted at the stage.

A tuft of red hair stuck up behind the green leaf.

"I think that's him behind the leaf," said his father doubtfully.

"I wonder why Henry is hiding," said Mom. "It's not like him to be shy."

"Hmmmm," said Dad.

"Shhh," hissed the parents beside them.

Henry watched the tomatoes and beans searching on tiptoe for the magic bananas.

I'm not staying back here, he thought, and pushed his way through the raindrops.

"Stop pushing, Henry!" hissed Lazy Linda.

Henry pushed harder, then did a few pitter-pats with the other raindrops.

Miss Tutu stretched out a bony arm and yanked Henry back behind the scenery.

Who wants to be a raindrop anyway, thought Henry. I can do what I like hidden here.

The tomatoes
weaved in and out,
twirling.

The beans
pirouetted.

The bananas
pointed their toes
and swayed.

The raindrops
pitter-patted.

Henry flapped his
arms and pretended
he was a *pterodactyl*
about to pounce on
Miss Tutu.

Round and round
he flew, homing in
on his prey.

Perfect Peter stepped
to the front and began
his solo.

Tap Tap Tap Tap Tap Tap—
CRASH!

One giant green leaf fell on top of the raindrops, knocking them over.

The raindrops collided with the tomatoes.

The tomatoes smashed into the string beans.

The string beans bumped into the bananas.

Perfect Peter turned his head to see what was happening and danced off the stage into the front row.

Miss Tutu fainted.

The only person still standing on stage was Henry.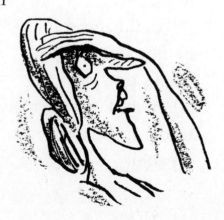

Stomp Stomp Stomp Stomp Stomp Stomp Stomp.

Henry did his
elephant dance.
   Boom Boom
Boom Boom Boom
Boom Boom.
   Henry did his
wild buffalo dance.

Peter tried to scramble back on stage.

The curtain fell.

There was a long silence, then Henry's parents clapped.

No one else did, so Henry's parents stopped.

All the other parents ran up to Miss Tutu and started shouting.

"I don't see why that horrid boy should have had such a long solo while all Linda did was lie on the floor," yelled one mother.

"My Jeffrey is a much better dancer than that boy," shouted another. "He should have done the solo."

"I didn't know you taught modern dance, Miss Tutu," said Violet's mother. "Come, Violet," she added, sweeping from the room.

"HENRY!!" screeched Miss Tutu. "Leave my dance studio at once!"

"Whoopee!" shouted Henry. He knew that next Saturday he would be at karate class at last.

HORRID HENRY'S SICK DAY

Cough! Cough!

Sneeze! Sneeze!

"Are you all right, Peter?" asked Mom.

Peter coughed, choked, and spluttered.

"I'm OK," he gasped.

"Are you sure?" said Dad. "You don't look very well."

"It's nothing," said Perfect Peter, coughing.

Mom felt Peter's sweaty brow.

"You've got a temperature," said Mom. "I think you'd better stay home from school today."

"But I don't want to miss school," said Peter.

"Go back to bed," said Mom.

"But I want to go to
school," wailed
Peter. "I'm sure I'll
be—" Peter's pale,
sweaty face turned
green. He dashed up the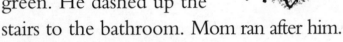
stairs to the bathroom. Mom ran after him.

Blecccccccchhhh. The horrible sound
of vomiting filled the house.

Horrid Henry stopped eating his toast.
Peter, stay at home? Peter, miss school?
Peter, lying around watching TV while he,
Henry, had to suffer a long hard day with
Miss Battle-Axe?

 No way! He was
sick too. Hadn't
he coughed
twice this
morning?
And he had
definitely sneezed

last night. Now that he thought about it, he could feel those flu germs invading. Yup, there they were, marching down his throat.

Stomp, stomp, stomp marched the germs. Mercy! shrieked his throat. Ha ha ha gloated the germs.

Horrid Henry thought about those spelling words he hadn't learned. The map he hadn't finished coloring. The book report he hadn't done.

Oww. His throat hurt.

Oooh. His tummy hurt.

Eeek. His head hurt.

Yippee! He was sick!

So what would it be?

Math or *Mutant Max*?

Reading or relaxing?

Commas or comics?

Tests or TV?

Hmmm, thought Horrid Henry. Hard choice.

Cough. Cough.

Dad continued reading the paper.

COUGH! COUGH! COUGH!
COUGH! COUGH!

"Are you all right, Henry?" asked
Dad, without looking up.

"No!" gasped Henry. "I'm sick too. I
can't go to school."

Slowly Dad put down his newspaper.

"You don't look ill, Henry," said Dad.

"But I am," whimpered Horrid
Henry. He clutched his throat. "My
throat really hurts," he moaned. Then
he added a few coughs, just in case.

"I feel weak," he groaned.
"Everything aches."

Dad sighed.

"All right, you can stay home," he said.

Yes! thought Horrid Henry. He was
amazed. It usually took much more
moaning and groaning before his mean,
horrible parents decided he was sick
enough to miss a day of school.

"But no playing on the computer," said Dad. "If you're sick, you have to lie down."

Horrid Henry was outraged.

"But it makes me feel better to play on the computer," he protested.

"If you're well enough to play on the computer, you're well enough to go to school," said Dad.

Rats.

Oh well, thought Horrid Henry. He'd get his blanket, lie on the sofa and watch lots of TV instead. Then Mom would

bring him cold drinks, lunch on a tray, maybe even ice cream. It was always such a waste when you were too sick to enjoy being sick, thought Horrid Henry happily.

He could hear Mom and Dad arguing upstairs.

"I need to go to work," said Mom.

"I need to go to work," said Dad.

"I stayed home last time," said Mom.

"No you didn't, I did," said Dad.

"Are you sure?" said Mom.

"Yes," said Dad.

"Are you sure you're sure?" said Mom.

Horrid Henry could hardly believe his ears. Imagine arguing over who got to stay home! When he was grown-up he was going to stay home full time, testing computer games for a million dollars a week.

He bounced into the sitting room. Then he stopped bouncing. A horrible, ugly, snotty creature was stretched out under a blanket in the comfy black chair. Horrid Henry glanced at the TV. A dreadful assortment of wobbling creatures were dancing and prancing.

TRA LA LA LA LA,
WE LIVE AT NELLIE'S
WE'VE ALL GOT BIG BELLIES
WE EAT PURPLE JELLIES
AT NELLIE'S NURSERY (tee-hee)

Horrid Henry sat down on the sofa.

"I want to watch *Robot Rebels*," said Henry.

"I'm watching *Nellie's Nursery*," said Peter, sniffing.

"Stop sniffing," said Henry.

"I can't help it, my nose is running," said Peter.

"I'm sicker than you, and I'm not sniffing," said Henry.

"I'm sicker than you," said Peter.

"Faker."

"Faker."

"Liar."

"Liar!"

"MOM!" shrieked Henry and Peter.

Mom came into the room, carrying a tray of cold drinks and two thermometers.

"Henry's being mean to me!" whined Peter.

"Peter's being mean to *me!*" whined Henry.

"If you're well enough to fight, you're well enough to go to school, Henry," said Mom, glaring at him.

"I wasn't fighting, Peter was," said Henry.

"Henry was," said Peter, coughing.

Henry coughed louder.

Peter groaned.

Henry groaned louder.

"Uggghhhh," moaned Peter.

"Uggghhhhhhhhh," moaned Henry.

"It's not fair. I want to watch *Robot Rebels*."

"I want to watch *Nellie's Nursery*," whimpered Peter.

"Peter will choose what to watch because he's the sickest," said Mom.

Peter, sicker than he was? As if. Well, no way was Henry's sick day going to be ruined by his horrible brother.

"I'm the sickest, Mom," protested Henry. "I just don't complain so much."

Mom looked tired. She popped one thermometer into Henry's mouth and the other into Peter's.

"I'll be back in five minutes to check them," she said. "And I don't want to hear another peep from either of you," she added, leaving the room.

Horrid Henry lay back weakly on the sofa with the thermometer in his mouth. He felt terrible. He touched his forehead. He was burning! His temperature must be 105!

I bet my temperature is so high the thermometer won't even have enough numbers, thought Henry. Just wait till Mom saw how ill he was. Then she'd be sorry she'd been so mean.

Perfect Peter started groaning. "I'm going to be sick," he gasped, taking the thermometer from his mouth and running from the room.

The moment Peter left, Henry leapt up from the sofa and checked Peter's thermometer. 101 degrees! Oh no, Peter had a temperature. Now Peter would start getting all the attention. Mom would make Henry fetch and carry for him. Peter might even get extra ice cream.

Something had to be done.

Quickly Henry plunged Peter's thermometer into the glass of iced water.

Beep. Beep. Horrid Henry took out his own thermometer. It read 98.6 degrees. Normal.

Normal! His temperature was normal? That was impossible. How could his temperature be normal when he was so ill?

If Mom saw that normal temperature she'd have him dressed for school in three seconds. Obviously there was something wrong with that stupid thermometer.

Horrid Henry held it to the light bulb. Just to warm it up a little, he thought.

Clump. Clump.

Yikes! Mom was coming back.

Quickly Henry yanked Peter's thermometer out of the iced water and replaced his own in his mouth. Oww! It was hot.

"Let's see if you have a temperature," said Mom. She took the thermometer out of Henry's mouth.

"127 degrees!" she shrieked.

Oops.

"The thermometer must be broken," mumbled Henry. "But I still have a temperature. I'm boiling."

"Hmm," said Mom, feeling Henry's forehead.

Peter came back into the sitting room slowly. His face was ashen.

"Check my temperature, Mom," said Peter. He lay back weakly on the pillows.

Mom checked Peter's thermometer.

"57 degrees!" she shrieked.

Oops, thought Horrid Henry.

"That one must be broken too," said Henry.

He decided to change the subject fast.

"Mom, could you open the curtains please?" said Henry.

"But I want them closed," said Peter.

"Open!"

"Closed!"

"We'll leave them closed," said Mom.

Peter sneezed.

"Mom!" wailed Henry. "Peter got snot all over me."

"Mom!" wailed Peter. "Henry's smelly."

Horrid Henry glared at Peter.

Perfect Peter glared at Henry.

Henry whistled.

Peter hummed.

"Henry's whistling!"

"Peter's humming!"

"MOM!" they screamed. "Make him stop!"

"That's enough!" shouted Mom. "Go to your bedrooms, both of you!"

Henry and Peter heaved their heavy bones upstairs to their rooms.

"It's all your fault," said Henry.

"It's yours," said Peter.

The front door opened. Dad came in. He looked pale.

"I'm not feeling well," said Dad. "I'm going to bed."

Horrid Henry was bored. Horrid Henry was fed up. What was the point of being sick if you couldn't watch TV and you couldn't play on the computer?

"I'm hungry!" complained Horrid Henry.

"I'm thirsty," complained Perfect Peter.

"I'm achy," complained Dad.

"My bed's too hot!" moaned Horrid Henry.

"My bed's too cold," moaned Perfect Peter.

"My bed's too hot and too cold," moaned Dad.

Mom ran up the stairs.

Mom ran down the stairs.

"Ice cream!" shouted Horrid Henry.

"Hot water bottle!" shouted Perfect Peter.

"More pillows!" shouted Dad.

Mom walked up the stairs.

Mom walked down the stairs.

"Toast!" shouted Henry.

"Tissues!" croaked Peter.

"Tea!" gasped Dad.

"Can you wait a minute?" said Mom. "I need to sit down."

"NO!" shouted Henry, Peter, and Dad.

"All right," said Mom.

She plodded up the stairs.

She plodded down the stairs.

"My head is hurting!"

"My throat is hurting!"

"My stomach is hurting!"

Mom trudged up the stairs.

Mom trudged down the stairs.

"Chips," screeched Henry.

"Throat lozenge," croaked Peter.

"Tissue," wheezed Dad.

Mom staggered up the stairs.

Mom staggered down the stairs.

Then Horrid Henry saw the time. Three thirty. School was finished! The weekend was here! It was amazing, thought Horrid Henry, how much better he suddenly felt.

Horrid Henry threw off his blanket and leaped out of bed.

"Mom!" he shouted. "I'm feeling much better. Can I go and play on the computer now?"

Mom staggered into his room.

"Thank goodness you're better, Henry," she whispered. "I feel terrible. I'm going to bed. Could you bring me a cup of tea?"

What?

"I'm busy," snapped Henry.

Mom glared at him.

"All right," said Henry, grudgingly. Why couldn't Mom get her own tea? She had legs, didn't she?

Horrid Henry escaped into the living room. He sat down at the computer and loaded "Intergalactic Robot Rebellion: This Time It's Personal." Bliss. He'd zap some robots, then have a go at "Snake Master's Revenge."

"Henry!" gasped Mom. "Where's my tea?"

"Henry!" rasped Dad. "Bring me a drink of water!"

"Henry!" whimpered Peter. "Bring me an extra blanket."

Horrid Henry scowled. Honestly, how was he meant to concentrate with all these interruptions?

"Tea!"

"Water!"

"Blanket!"

"Get it yourself!" he howled. What was he, a servant?

"Henry!" spluttered Dad. "Come up here this minute."

Slowly, Horrid Henry got to his feet. He looked longingly at the flashing screen. But what choice did he have?

"I'm sick too!" shrieked Horrid Henry. "I'm going back to bed."

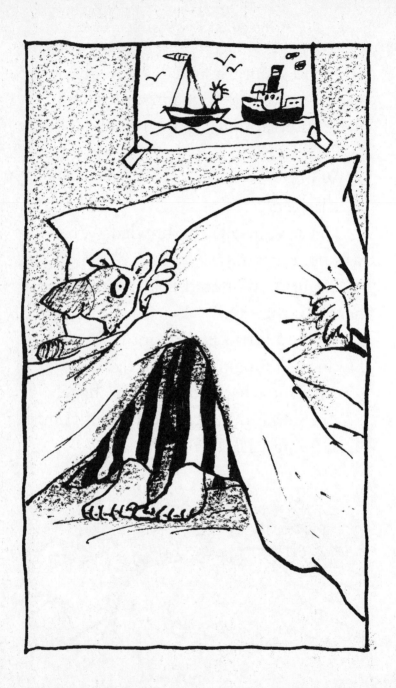

HORRID HENRY'S SWIMMING LESSON

Oh no! thought Horrid Henry. He pulled the blanket tightly over his head. It was Thursday. Horrible, horrible, Thursday. The worst day of the week. Horrid Henry was certain Thursdays came more often than any other day.

Thursday was his class swimming day. Henry had a nagging feeling that this Thursday was even worse than all the other awful Thursdays.

Horrid Henry liked the bus ride to
the pool. Horrid Henry liked doing
the dance of the seven towels in the
changing room. He also liked hiding in
the lockers, throwing socks in the pool,
and splashing everyone.

The only thing Henry didn't like about going swimming was…swimming.

The truth was, Horrid Henry hated water. Ugggh! Water was so…wet! And soggy. The chlorine stung his eyes. He never knew what horrors might be lurking in the deep end. And the pool was so cold penguins could fly in for the winter.

Fortunately, Henry had a brilliant list of excuses. He'd pretend he had warts, or a tummy ache, or had lost his swimsuit. Unfortunately, the mean, nasty, horrible swimming teacher, Soggy Sid, usually made him get in the pool anyway.

Then Henry would duck Dizzy Dave, or splash Weepy William, or pinch Gorgeous Gurinder, until Sid ordered him out. It was not surprising that Horrid Henry had never managed to get his five-meter badge.

Arrrgh! Now he remembered. Today was test day. The terrible day when everyone had to show how far they could swim. Aerobic Al was going for gold. Moody Margaret was going for silver. The only ones who were still trying for their five-meter badges were Lazy Linda and Horrid Henry. Five whole meters! How could anyone swim such a vast distance?

If only they were tested on who could sink to the bottom of the pool the fastest, or splash the most, or spit water the farthest, then Horrid Henry would have every badge in a jiffy. But no. He had to leap into a freezing cold pool, and, if he survived that shock, somehow thrash his way across five whole meters without drowning.

Well, there was no way he was going to school today.

Mom came into his room.

"I can't go to school today, Mom,"
Henry moaned. "I feel terrible."

Mom didn't even look at him.

"Thursday-itis again, I presume,"
said Mom.

"No way!" said Henry. "I didn't even
know it was Thursday."

"Get up, Henry," said Mom. "You're
going swimming and that's that."

Perfect Peter peeked around the door.

"It's badge day today!" he said. "I'm
going for fifty meters!"

"That's great, Peter," said Mom.
"I bet you're the best swimmer in
your class."

Perfect Peter smiled modestly.

"I just try my best," he said. "Good
luck with your five-meter badge,
Henry," he added.

Horrid Henry growled and attacked.

He was a Venus flytrap slowly
mashing a frantic fly between his
deadly leaves.

"Eeeeeowwww!" screeched Peter.

"Stop being horrid, Henry!" screamed
Mom. "Leave your poor brother
alone!"

Horrid Henry let Peter go. If only
he could find some way not to take his
swimming test he'd be the happiest boy
in the world.

Henry's class arrived at the pool. Okay, thought Henry. Time to unpack his excuses to Soggy Sid.

"I can't go swimming, I've got a wart," lied Henry.

"Take off your sock," ordered Soggy Sid.

Rats, thought Henry.

"Maybe it's better now," said Henry.

"I thought so," said Sid.

Horrid Henry grabbed his stomach.

"Tummy pains!" he moaned. "I feel terrible."

"You seemed fine when you were prancing around the pool a moment ago," snapped Sid. "Now get changed."

Time for the killer excuse.

"I forgot my swimsuit!" said Henry. This was his best chance of success.

"No problem," said Soggy Sid. He handed Henry a bag. "Put on one of these."

Slowly, Horrid Henry rummaged in the bag. He pulled out a bikini top, a blue suit with a hole in the middle, a pair of pink underpants, a tiny pair of green trunks, a polka-dot one piece with bunnies, see-through white shorts, and a diaper.

"I can't wear any of these!" protested Horrid Henry.

"You can and you will, if I have to put them on you myself," snarled Sid.

Horrid Henry squeezed into the green trunks. He could barely breathe. Slowly, he joined the rest of his class pushing and shoving by the side of the pool.

Everyone had millions of badges sewn all over their suits. You couldn't even see Aerobic Al's bathing suit beneath the stack of badges.

"Hey you!" shouted Soggy Sid. He pointed at Weepy William. "Where's your swimsuit?"

Weepy William glanced down and burst into tears.

"Waaaaah," he wailed and ran weeping back to the changing room.

"Now get in!" ordered Soggy Sid.

"But I'll drown!" screamed Henry. "I can't swim!"

"Get in!" screamed Soggy Sid.

Good-bye, cruel world. Horrid Henry held his breath and fell into the icy water. ARRRRGH! He was turning into an iceberg!

He was dying! He was dead! His feet flailed madly as he sank down, down, down—clunk! Henry's feet touched the bottom.

Henry stood up, choking and spluttering. He was waist-deep in water.

"Linda and Henry! Swim five meters—now!"

What am I going to do? thought Henry. It was so humiliating not even being able to swim five meters! Everyone would tease him. And he'd have to listen to them bragging about their badges! Wouldn't it be great to get a badge? Somehow?

Lazy Linda set off, very very slowly. Horrid Henry grabbed onto her leg. Maybe she'll pull me across, he thought.

"Ugggh!" gurgled Lazy Linda.

"Leave her alone!" shouted Sid. "Last chance, Henry."

Horrid Henry ran along the pool's bottom and flapped his arms, pretending to swim.

"Did it!" said Henry.

Soggy Sid scowled.

"I said swim, not walk!" screamed Sid. "You've failed. Now get over to the far lane and practice. Remember, anyone who stops swimming during the test doesn't get a badge."

Horrid Henry stomped over to the far lane. No way was he going to practice! How he hated swimming! He watched the others splashing up and down, up and down. There was Aerobic Al, doing his laps like a bolt of lightning. And Moody Margaret. And Kung-Fu Kate. Everyone would be getting a badge but Henry. It was so unfair.

"Pssst, Susan," said Henry. "Have you heard? There's a shark in the deep end!"

"Oh yeah, right," said Sour Susan.

She looked at the dark water in the far end of the pool.

"Don't believe me," said Henry. "Find out the hard way. Come back with a leg missing."

Sour Susan paused and whispered something to Moody Margaret.

"Shut up, Henry," said Margaret. They swam off.

"Don't worry about the shark, Andrew," said Henry. "I think he's already eaten today."

"What shark?" said Anxious Andrew.

Andrew stared at the deep end. It did look awfully dark down there.

"Start swimming, Andrew!" shouted Soggy Sid.

"I don't want to," said Andrew.

"Swim! Or I'll bite you myself!" snarled Sid.

Andrew started swimming.

"Dave, Ralph, Clare, and Bert—start swimming!" bellowed Soggy Sid.

"Look out for the shark!" said Horrid Henry. He watched Aerobic Al tearing up and down the lane. "Gotta swim, gotta swim, gotta swim," muttered Al between strokes.

What a show-off, thought Henry. Wouldn't it be fun to play a trick on him?

Horrid Henry pretended he was a crocodile. He sneaked under the water to the middle of the pool and waited until Aerobic Al swam overhead. Then Horrid Henry reached up.

Pinch! Henry grabbed Al's thrashing leg.

"AAAARGGG!" screamed Al. "Something's grabbed my leg. Help!" Aerobic Al leaped out of the pool.

Tee-hee, thought Horrid Henry.

"It's a shark!" screamed Sour Susan.
She scrambled out of the pool.

"There's a shark in the pool!"
screeched Anxious Andrew.

"There's a shark in the pool!" howled
Rude Ralph.

Everyone was screaming and shouting
and struggling to get out.

The only one left in the pool was
Henry.

Shark!

Horrid Henry forgot there were no
sharks in swimming pools.

Horrid Henry forgot *he'd* started the
shark rumor.

Horrid Henry forgot he couldn't swim.
All he knew was that he was alone in
the pool—with a shark!

Horrid Henry swam for his life.
Shaking and quaking, splashing and
crashing, he torpedoed his way to the
side of the pool and scrambled out.

He gasped and panted. Thank goodness. Safe at last! He'd never ever go swimming again.

"Five meters!" bellowed Soggy Sid. "You've all failed your badges today, except for—Henry!"

"Waaaaaaahhhhhh!" wailed the other children.

"Whoopee!" screamed Henry. "Olympics, here I come!"

HORRID HENRY
AND THE
SOCCER FIEND

....

"…AND with 15 seconds to go it's
Hot-Foot Henry racing across the
field! Beckham tries a slide tackle but
Henry's too quick! Just look at that step-
over! Oh no, he can't score from that
distance, it's crazy, it's impossible, oh my
goodness, he cornered the ball, it's IN!!!!
It's IN! Another *spectacular* goal! Another
spectacular win! And it's all thanks to
Hot-Foot Henry, the greatest soccer star
who's ever lived!"

"Goal! Goal! Goal!" roared the crowd. Hot-Foot Henry won the match! His teammates carried him through the fans, cheering and chanting, "Hen-ry! Hen-ry! Hen-ry!"

"HENRY!"

Horrid Henry looked up to see Miss Battle-Axe leaning over his table and glaring at him with her red eyes.

"What did I just say?"

"Henry," said Horrid Henry.

Miss Battle-Axe scowled.

"I'm watching you, Henry," she snapped. "Now class, please pay attention, we need to discuss—"

"Waaaaa!" wailed Weepy William.

"Susan, stop pulling my hair!" squealed Vain Violet.

"Miss!" shouted Inky Ian, "Ralph snatched my pen!"

"Did not!" shouted Rude Ralph.

"Did too!" shouted Inky Ian.

"Class! Be quiet!" bellowed Miss Battle-Axe.

"Waaaaa!" wailed Weepy William.

"Owwww!" squealed Vain Violet.

"Give it back!" shouted Inky Ian.

"Fine," said Miss Battle-Axe, "we won't talk about soccer."

William stopped wailing.

Violet stopped squealing.

Ian stopped shouting.

Henry stopped daydreaming.

Everyone in the class stared at Miss Battle-Axe. Miss Battle-Axe wanted to talk about…soccer? Was this an alien Miss Battle-Axe?

"As you all know, our local team, Ashton Athletic, has reached the sixth round of the National Soccer Cup," said Miss Battle-Axe.

"YAY!" shrieked the class.

"And I'm sure you all know what happened last night…"

Last night! Henry could still hear the announcer's glorious words as he and Peter had gathered around the radio as the draw for round six was announced.

"Number 16, Ashton Athletic, will be playing…" there was a long pause as the announcer drew another ball from the hat…"number 7, Manhattan United."

"Go Ashton!" shrieked Horrid Henry.

"As I was saying, before I was so rudely interrupted—" Miss Battle-Axe glared at Horrid Henry, "Ashton is playing Manhattan United in a few weeks. Every local elementary school has been given a pair of tickets. And thanks to my good luck in the teacher's draw, the lucky winner will come from our class."

"Me!" screamed Horrid Henry.

"Me!" screamed Moody Margaret.

"Me!" screamed Tough Toby, Aerobic Al, Fiery Fiona, and Brainy Brian.

"No one who shouts out will be getting anything," said Miss Battle-Axe. "Our class will be playing a soccer match at lunchtime. The best player of the match will win the tickets. I'm the referee and my decision will be final."

Horrid Henry was so stunned that for a moment he could scarcely breathe. National Soccer Cup tickets! National Soccer Cup tickets to see his local team Ashton play against Man U! Those tickets were like gold dust. Henry had begged and pleaded with Mom and

Dad to get tickets, but naturally they were all sold out by the time Henry's mean, horrible, lazy parents managed to heave their stupid bones to the phone. And now here was another chance to go to the match of the century!

Ashton Athletic had never got so far in the Cup. Sure, they'd knocked out the Tooting Tigers (chant: Toot Toot! Grrr!), the Pynchley Pythons, and the Cheam Champions but—Manhattan United! Henry had to go to the game. He just had to. And all he had to do was be MVP.

There was just one problem. Unfortunately, the best soccer player in the class wasn't Horrid Henry. Or Aerobic Al. Or Beefy Bert.

The best soccer player in the class was Moody Margaret. The second best player in the class was Moody Margaret.

The third best player in the class was
Moody Margaret. It was so unfair! Why
should Margaret of all people be so
fantastic at soccer?

Horrid Henry was great at shirt
pulling. Horrid Henry was superb at

screaming "Offside!" (whatever that meant). No one could howl "Come on, ref!" louder. And at toe treading, elbowing, barging, pushing, shoving, and tripping, Horrid Henry had no equal. The only thing Horrid Henry wasn't good at was playing soccer.

But never mind. Today would be different. Today he would dig deep inside and find the power to be Hot-Foot Henry—for real. Today no one would stop him. National Soccer Cup match here I come, thought Horrid Henry gleefully.

Lunchtime!

Horrid Henry's class dashed to the back playground, where the field was set up. Two sweatshirts at either end marked the goals. A few parents gathered on the sidelines.

Miss Battle-Axe split the class into two teams: Aerobic Al was captain of Henry's team, Moody Margaret was captain of the other.

There she stood in midfield, having nabbed a striker position, smirking confidently. Horrid Henry glared at her from the depths of the outfield.

"Na na ne nah nah, I'm sure to be MVP," trilled Moody Margaret, sticking out her tongue at him. "And you-ooo won't."

"Shut up, Margaret," said Henry. When he was king, anyone named Margaret would be boiled in oil and fed to the crows.

"Will you take me to the match, Margaret?" said Susan. "After all, *I'm* your best friend."

Moody Margaret scowled. "Since when?"

"Since always!" wailed Susan.

"Huh!" said Margaret. "We'll just have to see how nice you are to me, won't we?"

"Take me," begged Brainy Brian. "Remember how I helped you with those fractions?"

"And called me stupid," said Margaret.

"Did not," said Brian.

"Did too," said Margaret.

Horrid Henry eyed his classmates.
Everyone looking straight ahead,
everyone determined to be MVP.
Well, wouldn't they be in for a shock
when Horrid Henry waltzed off
with those tickets!

"Go Margaret!" screeched Moody
Margaret's mom.

"Go Al!" screeched Aerobic Al's dad.

"Everyone ready?" said Miss Battle-Axe.
"Bert! Which team are you on?"

"I dunno," said Beefy Bert.

Miss Battle-Axe blew her whistle.

Kick-off!

Kick.

Chase.

Kick.

Dribble.

Dribble.

Pass.

Kick.

Save!

Goal Kick.

Henry stood disconsolately on the left wing, running back and forth as the play passed him by. How could he ever be MVP stuck out here? Well, no way was he staying in this stupid spot a moment longer.

Horrid Henry abandoned his position and chased after the ball. All the other defenders followed him.

Moody Margaret had the ball. Horrid Henry ran up behind her. He glanced at Miss Battle-Axe. She was busy chatting to Mrs. Oddbod. Horrid Henry went for a two-foot slide tackle and tripped her.

"Foul!" screeched Margaret. "He hacked my leg!"

"Liar!" screeched Henry. "I just went for the ball!"

"Cheater!" screamed Moody Margaret's mom.

"Play on," ordered Miss Battle-Axe.

Yes! thought Horrid Henry triumphantly. After all, what did blind old Miss Battle-Axe know about the rules of soccer? Nothing. This was his golden chance to score.

Now Jazzy Jim had the ball.

Horrid Henry stepped on his toes, elbowed him, and grabbed the ball.

"Hey, we're on the same team!" yelped Jim.

Horrid Henry kept dribbling.

"Pass! Pass!" screamed Al. "I'm open!"

Henry ignored him. Pass the ball? Was Al crazy? For once Henry had the ball and he was keeping it.

Then suddenly Moody Margaret
appeared from behind, barged him,
dribbled the ball past Henry's team,
and kicked it straight past Weepy
William into the goal. Moody
Margaret's team cheered.

Weepy William burst into tears.

"Waaaaaa," wailed Weepy William.

"Idiot!" screamed Aerobic Al's dad.

"She cheated!" shrieked Henry. "She
fouled me!"

"Did not," said Margaret.

"How dare you call my daughter a
cheater?" screamed
Margaret's mom.

Miss Battle-Axe
blew her whistle.

"Goal to
Margaret's team.
The score is one–
nothing."

Horrid Henry gritted his teeth. He would score a goal if he had to trample on every player to do so.

Unfortunately, everyone else seemed to have the same idea.

"Ralph pushed me!" shrieked Aerobic Al.

"Did not!" lied Rude Ralph. "It was just an accident."

"He used his hands; I saw him!" howled Al's father. "Send him off."

"I'll send *you* off if you don't behave," snapped Miss Battle-Axe, looking up and blowing her whistle.

"It was kept in!" protested Henry.

"No way!" shouted Margaret. "It went past the line!"

"That was ball to hand!" yelled Kind Kasim.

"No way!" screamed Aerobic Al. "I just went for the ball."

"Liar!"

"Liar!"

"Free kick to Margaret's team," said Miss Battle-Axe.

"Ouch!" screamed Soraya, as Brian stepped on her toes, grabbed the ball, and headed it into the goal past Kasim.

"Hurray!" cheered Al's team.

"Foul!" screamed Margaret's team.

"Score is one all," said Miss Battle-Axe. "Five more minutes to go."

AAARRRGGHH! thought Horrid Henry. I've got to score a goal to have a chance to be MVP. I've just got to. But how, how?

Henry glanced at Miss Battle-Axe. She appeared to be rummaging in her purse. Henry saw his chance. He stuck out his foot as Margaret hurtled past.

Crash!

Margaret tumbled.

Henry seized the ball.

"Henry kicked my leg!" shrieked Margaret.

"Did not!" shrieked Henry. "I just went for the ball."

"REF!" screamed Margaret.

"He cheated!" screamed Margaret's mom. "Are you blind, ref?"

Miss Battle-Axe glared.

"My eyesight is perfect, thank you," she snapped.

Tee-hee, chortled Horrid Henry.

Henry stepped on Brian's toes, elbowed him, then grabbed the ball. Then Dave elbowed Henry, Ralph trod on Dave's toes, and Susan seized the ball and kicked it high overhead.

Henry looked up. The ball was high, high
up. He'd never reach it, not unless, unless—
Henry glanced at Miss Battle-Axe. She
was watching a traffic officer patrolling
outside the school gate. Henry leapt
into the air and whacked the ball with
his hand.

Thwack!

The ball hurled across the goal.

"Goal!" screamed Henry.

"He used his hands!" protested Margaret.

"No way!" shouted Henry. "It was the hand of God!"

"Henry! Henry! Hen-ry!" cheered his team.

"Unfair!" howled Margaret's team.

Miss Battle-Axe blew her whistle.

"Time!" she bellowed. "Al's team wins 2–1."

"Yes!" shrieked Horrid Henry, punching the air. He'd scored the winning goal! He'd be MVP! Ashton Athletic versus Man U, here I come!

★ ★ ★

Horrid Henry's class limped through the door and sat down. Horrid Henry sat at the front, beaming. Miss Battle-Axe had to award him the tickets after his brilliant performance and spectacular, game-winning goal. The question was, who *deserved* to be his guest?

No one.

I know, thought Horrid Henry, I'll sell my other ticket. Bet I get a million dollars for it. No, a billion dollars. Then I'll buy my own team, and play striker any time I want to. Horrid Henry smiled happily.

Miss Battle-Axe glared at her class.

"That was abso-lutely disgraceful," she said. "Cheating! Moving the goals!

Shirt tugging!" she glared at Graham. "Pushing!"

She glowered at Ralph. "Pushing and shoving! Bad sportsmanship!" Her eyes swept over the class.

Horrid Henry sank lower in his seat. Oops.

"And don't get me started about the offsides penalties," she snapped.

Horrid Henry sank even lower.

"There was only one person who deserves to be MVP," she continued. "One person who observed the rules of the beautiful game. One person who has nothing to be ashamed of today."

Horrid Henry's heart leapt. *He* certainly had nothing to be ashamed of.

"…One person who can truly be proud of his or her performance…"

Horrid Henry beamed with pride.

"And that person is—"

"Me!" screamed Moody Margaret.

"Me!" screamed Aerobic Al.

"Me!" screamed Horrid Henry.

"—the referee," said Miss Battle-Axe.

What?

Miss Battle-Axe...MVP?

Miss Battle-Axe...a soccer fiend?

"IT's NOT FAIR!" screamed the class.

"IT's NOT FAIR!" screamed Horrid Henry.

And now it's time for some fun! Let's get started!

Sports Search

Can you find all of the sports listed below in the word search? The words are printed forward, backward, up, down, and diagonally.

SOCCER
BASKETBALL
FOOTBALL
BASEBALL
TENNIS
SWIMMING
HOCKEY
GOLF
VOLLEYBALL

V	Y	E	K	C	O	H	Z	R	B
P	O	S	W	I	M	M	I	N	G
I	Y	L	U	E	A	Y	G	B	F
S	G	E	L	T	K	J	O	H	O
O	B	A	S	E	B	A	L	L	O
C	Y	T	P	N	Y	T	F	O	T
C	Z	A	R	N	X	B	U	C	B
E	L	B	C	I	A	H	A	F	A
R	O	Y	K	S	J	E	Z	L	L
B	A	S	K	E	T	B	A	L	L

Unscramble the Tiles

Can you rearrange the tower of tiles to reveal something that Horrid Henry's mom and dad are always saying to him? Make sure you match up the colors in the tower with the colors in the answer tiles.

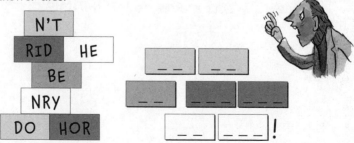

N'T
RID   HE
BE
NRY
DO   HOR

Alliteration & Adjectives

AL•LIT•ER•A•TION

When words repeat the same beginning sound, like a tongue twister!
Example: Sally sells seashells by the seashore.

Horrid Henry, Perfect Peter, and Moody Margaret are characters in our books, and their names all use alliteration.

AD•JEC•TIVES

Words that describe people, places, or things.
Examples: Happy, tall, young, small.

The names in Horrid Henry use adjectives to describe characters. The word "perfect" describes Peter because he is so good! The word "moody" describes Margaret because she gets grumpy ALL THE TIME!

Make up your own Horrid Henry character name!

Can you think of a Horrid Henry character name
for yourself that uses alliteration and adjectives?

_____

Why did you pick this name for yourself?

_____

_____

Why would you get along with Horrid Henry?

_____

_____

_____

Why wouldn't you get along with Horrid Henry?

_____

_____

_____

uNderpaNts!

Great-Aunt Greta sent Horrid Henry a disgusting pair of pink lacy underpants decorated with glittery hearts and bows for his birthday. But the worst part was that Henry accidentally wore those frilly underpants to school! What could be worse?

See if you can come up with a pair of underpants that is weirder, uglier, or wilder than what Henry had to wear!

Draw a picture of your underpants design here!

An Author Visit with Horrid Henry

If you could have any author visit your class, who would it be?

_____

Would Horrid Henry like your author visit? Why or why not?

_____

_____

_____

What kind of mischief would Horrid Henry cause at your author visit?

_____

_____

_____

_____

_____

An Author Visit with Horrid Henry

Draw a picture of Horrid Henry making mischief at your author visit.

Draw your picture here.

My Favorite Books!

What is your favorite book that you have read in school?

_____

What is your favorite book to read at home?

_____

Who do you talk to about your favorite books?

_____

_____

_____

_____

_____

_____

Draw your own
Horrid Henry book cover!

Draw your own book cover design for *Horrid Henry's Author Visit* here:

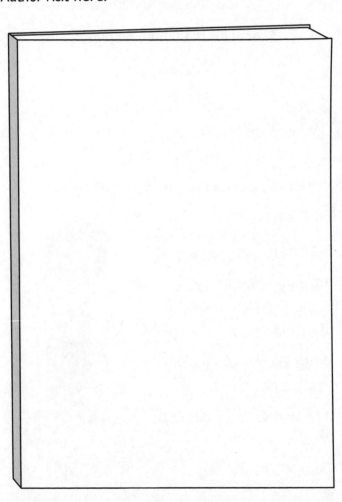

Horrid Henry's School Jokes

What's the difference between school lunches and slugs?

School lunches come on plates.

What's the difference between homework and an onion?

Nobody cries when you cut up homework.

Henry: Would you blame someone for something they didn't do?

Miss Battle-Axe: Of course not.

Henry: Good, I didn't do my homework.

write your favorite joke here:

_____

_____

_____

Draw a picture to go along with your joke.

Perfect Peter's Diary

Horrid Henry tried to fix Perfect Peter's diary to make it less boring. But Horrid Henry made some spelling mistakes. Can you find the words that are spelled wrong and fix them?

MONDAY

Today I drew a picture of my teacher, Miss Lovely. I drew her with piggy ears and a grate big giant belly. Then I turned it into a dartboard. Miss Lovely gave me a gold star for reading. Miss Lovely is my worst teecher ever. She should reely be called Miss Lumpy. Miss Dumpy Lumpy is wot Gordon and I call her behind her back. Tee hee, she'll never know! I'm the best reader in the class. And the best at math. And the best at everything else. Too bad I have smelly pants and dirty hair.

TUESDAY

Today I said please and thank you 236 times. Not!! I called Mom a big blobby pants face. I called Dad a stinky fish. Then I played Pirats with the world's greatest brother, Henry. I wish I were as smart as Henry. But I know that's impossibel.

Note: answers printed upside down

ANSWERS: Monday: grate – great; reely – really; teecher – teacher; wot – what; **Tuesday:** Pirats – Pirates; impossibel – impossible; Wenesday;Wenesday – Wednesday; reelly – really; bruther – brother; Thursday; no errors; Friday; no errors

WENESDAY

Today I sharpened my pencils. All the better to write rude notes! I ate all my sprouts and had seconds. Then threw up all over Mom. Eeugh, what a smell. I reelly am a smelly toad. I am so lucky to have a great bruther like Henry. He is always so nice to me. Hip Hip Hurray for Henry

THURSDAY

Today I ate all my vegetables.

_____

_____

_____

_____

_____

_____

_____

FRIDAY

Today I wrote a poem to my bottom
I love my bottom
I want to wave a pom-pom
I love my bottom

Write your own additions to Perfect Peter's diary on the lines above.

Treasure Hunt

Horrid Henry wants to be a pirate. Draw a line through the maze to help Horrid Henry find the pirate's treasure!

Untangle the Mess!

Horrid Henry made his own comic book about his favorite character, Skeleton Skunk, to bring to school. But it's lost in his messy room! Can you help him find it?

Coloring Fun!

Horrid Henry and Perfect Peter

Coloring Fun!

Moody Margaret

Even More Jokes!

Margaret: Knock knock.

Susan: Who's there?

Margaret: Cows go.

Susan: Cows go who?

Margaret: No they don't, they go moo.

What's brown and sticky?

A brown stick.

What has eighteen legs and catches flies?

A baseball team.

which Perfect Peter isn't perfect?

All of these pictures of Perfect Peter look exactly alike.
But one of them is different! Can you find the mistake?

You can make your own GLOP!

It's very simple to make your own disgusting, gooey, gross Glop. You can make Glop with anything you can find in the kitchen—the yuckier the better! Horrid Henry and Moody Margaret mixed oatmeal, vinegar, baked beans, moldy cheese, and even peanut butter into their icky Glop. If you want to make some simple Glop, try this basic recipe.

Ingredients

16 oz box of cornstarch

1 ½ cups water

Food coloring (optional)

Directions

Dump the cornstarch and water into a large bowl. Add about 15 or 20 drops of food coloring. Squish the Glop together with your hands until it's all mixed. Now gross out your little brother or sister by letting the Glop ooze through your fingers! Yuck!

What will you put in your Glop? Horrid Henry's rules are to use only things you can find in the kitchen. On the lines below, write all the gross things you could use to make your Glop.

_____

_____

_____

_____

_____

_____

_____

_____

_____

_____

Have you read all the Horrid Henry books?

Draw a circle around the books you want to read.

Draw a square around the books that you have read.

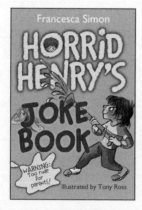